For Peggy Sharkey

SCRIBNER
1230 Avenue of the Americas
New York, NY 10020

SCRIBNER and design are trademarks of
Macmillan Library Reference USA, Inc., used under license
by Simon & Schuster, the publisher of this work.

For information about special discounts for bulk purchases,
please contact Simon & Schuster Special Sales:
1-800-456-6798 or business@simonandschuster.com

Text set in Sabon

Manufactured in the United States of America

1   3   5   7   9   10   8   6   4   2

Library of Congress Cataloging-in-Publication Data
Connors, Rose.
False testimony / Rose Connors.
p. cm.
I. Title.
PS3603.O553F35 2005
813'.6—dc22   2005045052

ISBN-13: 978-0-7432-6197-5
ISBN-10:   0-7432-6197-6

FALSE TESTIMONY

ROSE CONNORS

SCRIBNER

New York   London   Toronto   Sydney

ACKNOWLEDGMENTS

Sincere thanks to the literary dream team: my editor, Sarah Knight, and my agent, Nancy Yost.

Thanks also to those individuals who contributed generously to the Cape Cod & Islands United Way in exchange for the right to christen a character.

And finally, thanks to the members of my weekly writing circle: Sara Young, Pauline Grocki, Penny Haughwout, and Maureen Hourihan—wordsmiths one and all.

FALSE
TESTIMONY

Massachusetts Rules
of Professional Conduct

Rule 3.3—Candor Toward the Tribunal

(e) In a criminal case, if defense counsel . . . knows that the client has testified falsely, the lawyer shall call upon the client to rectify the false testimony and, if the client refuses or is unable to do so, the lawyer shall not reveal the false testimony to the tribunal.

CHAPTER I

Monday, December 13

A person of interest. That's what local authorities dubbed Charles Kendrick, the senior United States Senator from the Commonwealth of Massachusetts. He wasn't a target of the investigation, they told him. He was merely an individual believed to have information relevant to the search.

And he did. Twenty-five-year-old Michelle Forrester was a member of his D.C. staff. He hired her more than three years ago, just after she graduated from the University of Virginia with dual degrees in government science and drama. An ambitious and disarmingly attractive young woman with obvious political aspirations of her own, she quickly became Senator Kendrick's preferred spokesperson. For the past year—while rumors ran rampant about his planned bid for the Democratic nomination—Michelle Forrester alone fielded questions at his frequent public appearances. She enabled the Senator to say his piece at each event and then make a dignified—perhaps even presidential—exit.

This past Thursday, Michelle handled the members of the media after the Senator addressed a standing-room-only crowd at Cape Cod Community College in Hyannis. The evening news featured a poised and charming Michelle entertaining endless inquiries from local reporters, joking and laughing with them easily and often. She stayed until their voracious journalists' appetites were satisfied, until the last of their detailed and often repetitive questions was answered. She extended Senator Kendrick's sincere thanks to all of them, for their attendance and their attention, before she left the auditorium.

And then Michelle Forrester vanished.

She was due at her parents' home in Stamford, Connecticut, the next day to help with preparations for a cocktail party to be held that evening in honor of her father's sixtieth birthday. She didn't show up—not for the preparations and not for the party. She was expected back at work in D.C. first thing this morning, her office calendar jammed with appointments from eight o'clock on. She didn't show there, either. And though her worried parents had been calling both Massachusetts and Connecticut authorities all weekend, it wasn't until her no-show at work that the search began in earnest.

Postpone it. That's what I advised when Senator Kendrick called my office at ten A.M. He'd stayed on the Cape after Thursday's speech, intending to work by phone and fax through the holidays from his vacation home in North Chatham. The Barnstable County District Attorney's Office called his D.C. number first thing this morning and his executive secretary phoned him right away with the message. It was from Geraldine Schilling—the District Attorney herself—wanting to set up a time when she might ask him a few questions. Today, if at all possible.

Senator Kendrick made it clear to me from the outset that he wasn't seeking formal representation. He simply wanted to know if one of the lawyers in our office would be available by telephone later in the morning in case he needed a word of advice during his interview. He didn't anticipate a problem, he assured me more than once. He was calling only out of an abundance of caution.

Twenty-four hours, I told him. Of course you'll cooperate with the investigation, and of course you'll do it promptly; time is paramount in these matters. But you shouldn't speak to the DA—or to any other representative of the Commonwealth, for that matter—without an attorney at your side. He was quick to inform me that he *is* an attorney—Harvard-trained, he added—whereupon I recited my personal version of the old adage: Never mind the fool; the lawyer who represents himself has a certifiable moron for a client.

Answer questions tomorrow, I urged. Spend this afternoon in my office, preparing, and we'll go to the District Attorney together in the morning. That way, if her questioning takes a direction it shouldn't, I'll be the one to hit the brakes. You'll remain the willing witness, reluctantly accepting advice from your overly protective attorney.

Senator Kendrick's laughter took me by surprise. I wasn't trying to be funny. After a good chuckle, he thanked me for my time. And before I could answer, I was listening to a dial tone.

CHAPTER 2

"Good of you to join us, Martha." Geraldine Schilling is the only person on the planet who calls me Martha. And she knows damned well I'm not here to join anybody. Charles Kendrick called me a second time—ten minutes ago, at one-thirty—because he's worried. And he should be.

"Party's over, Geraldine. No more questions."

"Attorney Nickerson can be a bit rude." Geraldine presses an index finger to her cheek and directs her observation exclusively to Senator Kendrick, as though I'm not in the room. "I should have trained her better," she adds. She sounds almost apologetic.

Geraldine "trained" me for a solid decade, when I was an ADA and she was the First Assistant. If she'd done the job as she intended, I'd be a hell of a lot worse than rude. I'd also still be a prosecutor, not a member of the defense bar. I lift her black winter coat from the back of an upholstered wing chair in the corner and hold it out, letting it dangle from two fingers. "Adios," I tell her. "You're done here."

She accepts the heavy coat but doesn't put it on. Instead, she takes a pack of Virginia Slims from its inside pocket and then drapes it over her arm. She tamps a beige cigarette from the pack, shakes her long blond bangs at me, then turns to the Senator and arches her pale eyebrows. She seems to think he might override my decision. She's mistaken, though; she trained me better than that.

"You're done," I repeat. "Senator Kendrick spoke with you voluntarily this morning but he's not doing that anymore. Not at the moment, anyway. He called his attorney. That's me. This is his home. And I've asked you to leave."

"Marty, is that really necessary?" Senator Kendrick is seated on his living room couch, a deep-maroon, soft leather sectional. Behind him, through the floor-to-ceiling windows, is a heart-stopping view of the winter Atlantic. His long legs are crossed—in perfectly creased blue jeans—and his starched, white dress shirt is open at the collar, sleeves rolled up to the middle of his forearms. His gray-blue eyes mirror the choppy surf, yet he seems far more relaxed than he should be under the circumstances.

"Take a look outside," I tell him, pointing to a pair of mullioned windows that face the driveway. "And then you tell me if it's necessary."

He stands, sighing and looking taxed by the effort, and crosses the antique Oriental carpet to the dark, polished hardwood at the perimeter of the vast room. I follow and stop just a few steps behind him, eyeing his chiseled profile as he parts the curtains and leans on the sill. He's silent for a moment as he gets a gander of the scene that greeted me when I arrived. "Standard procedure?" he asks at last.

"Not even close," I tell him.

Four vehicles occupy the crushed-shell driveway, all facing the closed doors of the dormered, three-car garage. The shiny Buick is Geraldine's; she gets a new one every two years without fail, always dark blue. The ancient Thunderbird in desperate need of a trip to the car wash is mine. The enormous gray Humvee, I can only presume, is the Senator's. And the patrol car belongs to the Town of Chatham. Two uniforms stand in front of it, leaning against its hood and talking, their breath making small white clouds in the cold December air.

The Kendrick estate sits on a point, a narrow spit of land that juts out into the Atlantic. It has a solitary neighbor, a small bungalow, to the north. Otherwise, the Kendricks enjoy exclusive use of this strip, the front and sides of their spacious house bordered by nothing but open ocean. The cops are in the driveway for a reason, not passing through on their way to someplace else. The Kendrick estate isn't on the way to anyplace else.

"The one closest to us is the Chief," I tell the Senator. "Ten bucks says he'll shoot the lock off your front door if your friend the DA here presses the right button on her pager."

Senator Kendrick pulls the curtains back together and turns away from the windows to face Geraldine. She dons her coat as she stares back at him, transferring her still unlit cigarette from one hand to the other as she threads her arms through the coat's tailored sleeves. "Senator," she snaps, her tone altogether different than it was just moments ago.

He stiffens beside me and turns my way, but I stare at Geraldine as her deep green eyes bore into him. "We've barely begun to check out your story," she says, "and already, parts of it don't fly."

He takes a step toward me but still I don't look at him. Since

I'm the only person in this room who hasn't heard his story, there's not a hell of a lot I can offer.

"That can't be," he says.

"Shut up, Senator." The utter shock of my command renders him compliant—for the moment, at least. Still, I keep my eyes fixed on our District Attorney. She carries little more than a hundred pounds on her five-foot-two-inch frame, but there's not a tougher DA in the Commonwealth. Geraldine Schilling is no lightweight.

I take my cell phone from my jacket pocket and flip it open as I walk toward the kitchen—and Geraldine. "At this point," I tell her, "you're nothing more than a common trespasser."

She laughs.

"And *I've* got the Chief on speed-dial too."

She laughs again, louder this time, but she moves toward the kitchen door. She pauses, digs out a lighter from her coat pocket, and ignites the tip of the cigarette now pressed between her well-glossed lips. She opens the inner door, sucks in a long drag as she reaches for the outer one, and then blows a steady stream of smoke over her shoulder, her smoldering green eyes moving from mine to the Senator's. "Mark my words," she says to both of us. "I'll be back."

CHAPTER 3

"How's Chuck?" Harry stares at the snowy road ahead as he asks, a small smile tugging at the corners of his lips. He apparently finds it amusing that the Commonwealth's senior senator is proving to be a less-than-model client.

"*Chuck* is the same as he was this morning," I tell him. "Difficult." I flip the heater in Harry's old Jeep up another couple of notches and shift in the passenger seat to face him. He's driving with one gloved hand, clutching a cardboard cup of steaming coffee with the other.

"Makes sense," he says. "The guy's usually the one calling the shots; he isn't used to taking orders."

"I'm not issuing orders, Harry. I'm offering advice."

He smiles at me and then swallows a mouthful of coffee. "And you're just the drill sergeant for the job." He laughs.

Now there's a sentiment every forty-something woman hopes to hear from the man in her life.

It's three o'clock and we're pulling into the Barnstable County Complex, headed up the hill to the House of Correction. We'll spend the next couple of hours with Derrick Holliston, a twenty-two-year-old creep who's accused of murdering a popular parish priest last Christmas Eve. Harry is Holliston's court-appointed defender and—according to Harry—neither of them is happy about it. Holliston apparently thinks Harry's efforts are less than zealous. And Harry calls Holliston a lowlife, a bottom-feeder.

Like it or not, Harry and I will spend the rest of the afternoon walking Holliston through his direct testimony. Tomorrow, to the extent possible, we'll prepare him for cross. His first-degree-murder trial starts Wednesday morning. And unless Harry can convince him otherwise in the next forty-eight hours, Holliston intends to take the stand. He plans to tell the judge and jury that he acted in self-defense; that fifty-seven-year-old Father Frank McMahon made aggressive sexual advances toward him on the evening in question; that when Holliston resisted, the older man became violent. If Harry's instincts are on target—and I've never known them to be otherwise—Holliston's story is just that. Fiction.

Harry pulls into a snow-clogged spot and parks near the steps leading up to the foreboding House of Correction. He leaves the engine running, though, and shifts in his seat to lean against the driver's side door. It seems he intends to finish his coffee before we go inside. "The guy's a liar," he says.

"You don't know that, Harry. You think he's lying, but you don't know it." Harry and I have had this discussion a hundred times over the course of the past year, but he can't let it go. It's eating at him.

"Trust me," he says. "I know."

"No, you don't. Not the way the Rules of Professional Conduct require. There were two people in St. Veronica's Chapel when it happened. One of them is dead. Holliston is the only living person who was there. No one can prove he's lying."

Harry shakes his head and stares into his coffee cup. He's struggling with the ugly issue that confronts every criminal defense lawyer sooner or later: what to do when you believe—but can't prove—your client's story is fabricated. If he could prove it—before Holliston testifies—he could move for permission to withdraw from the case completely. His motion wouldn't necessarily be granted, but at least he'd have a shot. As it stands, with nothing but his gut telling him his client's a liar, he's stuck. And once Holliston testifies, Harry will be stuck for good. At that point, even if he were to discover slam-dunk evidence of perjury, he'd be obligated to keep it to himself. The Massachusetts Canons of Professional Ethics say so.

Harry stares through the now foggy windshield and his eyes settle on the chain-link fence surrounding the House of Correction. The fence is twenty feet high—twenty-two if you count the electrified barbed wire coiled at the top—but Harry doesn't seem to see an inch of it. He's preoccupied, brooding even. And I don't need a crystal ball to tell me his thoughts are back in Chatham, in the center of the small sacristy at St. Veronica's Chapel.

"I can prove Holliston's lying," he says, still staring uphill. "Give me fifteen minutes alone with him—in a dark alley."

"Listen to yourself, Harry. If you ever got wind of a cop saying something like that, you'd call him a miscreant. You'd raise the courthouse roof to suppress his testimony. And then you'd go after his badge."

13

Harry nods, conceding all points, and drains the last of his coffee. "Come on," he says, dropping the empty cup into a plastic bag dangling from the cigarette lighter. "Let's get this over with."

We emerge into the late-day mist and both lock our doors before slamming them shut. Most of the time, Harry doesn't bother to lock his Jeep. Any thief dumb enough to steal this crate deserves to drive it for a while, he always says. But here in the county complex the rules are different. Harry locks without fail, not because he's more concerned about car theft here than anywhere else, but because he'd rather not have an unexpected visitor waiting in the backseat when he returns.

The stone steps are covered with snow that melted a little during yesterday's foray into above-freezing temperatures and then refroze during last night's return to single digits. I opt to climb the hill beside the steps instead, where my boots can find a little traction in the snow. Harry trudges up the hill too, on the opposite side of the stairs, though he seems oblivious to the icy conditions. He looks down at the shin-high snow, one hand clutching the battered schoolbag he carries in lieu of a briefcase, the other tucked into his coat pocket. "So what did you tell old Chuck?" he asks, glancing sideways at me. "What are his marching orders?"

"I didn't give him marching orders, Harry."

"Oh, right." He removes his free hand from his pocket and taps his temple. "Advice," he says, feigning the utmost seriousness. "You gave him lawyerly advice. What was it?"

At six feet, 210, Harry has a good half foot and ninety pounds on me. But I'd like to clock him upside the head anyway. "Simple," I say. "I told our senior senator to keep his mouth shut."

Harry laughs out loud, sending a cloud of white vapor into the cold air ahead of us. "Simple? Are you serious, Marty? The guy's been a politician his entire adult life. You think it's going to be simple for him to keep his mouth shut?"

I walk ahead of Harry as the guard at the front booth presses a button that opens the prison's enormous double doors, two slabs of black steel in the center of a redbrick mountain. "It better be," I answer over my shoulder. "The guy's front and center in a high-profile missing person case. And the young woman's been gone four days now. He damn well better keep his mouth shut."

The front desk is manned by two guards who would look ominous even without their shiny weapons. They greet us with silent nods and wait, knowing we'll jump through the institutional hoops without instruction. We hand over our Massachusetts Bar cards to be checked against the list of warden-approved appointments. We empty our pockets of keys, paper clips, and coins. We turn in our coats, hats, and gloves. I surrender my Lady Smith as well and Harry pulls Derrick Holliston's thick file from the old schoolbag. The file goes in with us; the bag stays here.

Once each of us is stripped to a single layer of clothes, we're directed—one at a time—through the metal detector beside the desk. Neither of us sets if off, which comes as a great shock to everyone in the room. This particular machine usually shrieks at all of us—for no apparent reason. A third guard meets us on the other side of it, his expression wary. He looks like he's about fifteen and his eyes say he's already made up his mind about Harry and me. Our failure to set off the alarm renders us suspect.

We wait with the vigilant guard—our assigned escort, I presume—while the two at the front desk rummage through Holliston's file. They seem to think we might have hidden something sinister amid our pretrial motions. A miniature hacksaw, perhaps, along with a diagram of the escape route voted most likely to succeed by the county's cleverest guests. Minutes pass before they apparently conclude that the overstuffed accordion folder holds nothing of interest. They turn it over to the cautious one, who directs us toward the dingy corridor behind him with a toss of his crew-cut head.

Harry and I lead the way, our escort three paces behind with the file tucked under one arm. "Stop right there," he orders soon after we pass the first door on our left. We do, knowing he allowed us to walk past our destination on purpose. It's a device some of them use—mostly the new guys—to avoid ever turning their backs to their charges, no matter who their charges happen to be. His key is already in the lock when we turn to face him. He keeps his focus on us as he opens the door and steps aside. He hands the file to Harry when we approach and Harry enters the meeting room first. As I follow, the young guard assumes a sentinel's pose in the hallway and gives me a gentlemanly nod.

Our client is already here. Derrick Holliston is seated at a small, banged-up card table and I'm initially surprised to see he's free of restraints. I shouldn't be, though. This eight-by-ten room is windowless—the air in it long past stale—and its solitary door locks automatically. The accused isn't going anywhere.

Harry drops the heavy file onto the table and roots through his jacket pockets until he comes up with his glasses. "This is Marty Nickerson," he says to Holliston as he puts them on. "She'll sit second-chair at trial."

Harry and I frequently second-chair for each other. Limited resources dictate that only one of us actively works each file, but when a trial rolls around, an extra set of eyes and ears can be critical. The second chair also takes a witness or two in most cases, giving lead counsel a much-needed breather. We've decided I'll handle Tommy Fitzpatrick in this one. He's Chatham's Chief of Police. And I was an ADA long enough to establish a pretty good rapport with him.

Holliston stares at me for a moment, then turns his attention back to Harry. "Good," the less-than-satisfied client says. "You need help."

Harry looks over his glasses at Holliston and smirks, but otherwise lets the remark pass. He sits and starts unpacking the file without a word. I retrieve my own glasses from my jacket pocket and then claim the only remaining seat.

"First of all," Harry says, opening a manila folder in the middle of the table, "let's go over the Commonwealth's offer again."

"Let's not," Holliston says, mimicking Harry's cadence. "Let's tell the Commonwealth to stick its lousy offer where the sun don't shine. I told you—I ain't doin' time. Not for this one."

Harry leans back on two legs of his chair. "You are if you're convicted," he says evenly, "You're doing endless time."

"Well, now, that's where you come in, ain't it? You got a job to do, remember? You're the guy whose job is to get me off."

On the surface, Harry appears entirely unaffected by his client's comments. But I know better. He'd like to deck this smart-ass.

"I'm also the guy who's supposed to advise you," he says, his words measured. "And I'm advising you to seriously consider pleading out."

"Yeah? Well, you can stick your advice right up there with the offer." Holliston stands, folds his arms against the chest of his orange jumpsuit, and presses his back against the wall. He's a wiry man, five-ten or so, with a sketchy mustache and greasy brown hair that hangs below his collar. His pallid complexion is partially covered by a five o'clock shadow—yesterday's and today's, I'm guessing. "I told you a hundred times," he says, jutting his chin out at Harry. "No deal. What're you, deaf?"

Holliston reaches up to the low, suspended ceiling and dislodges one fiberglass square. He peers into the opening, presumably expecting to find the treasure he stashed up there the last time he was here.

"Did you lose something?" Harry asks.

Holliston glares at him like an impudent child. "No, I dint *lose* nothing," he says. He goes back to examining the gap he created, appearing to be in no hurry to continue our discussion. "I was an electrician in a prior life," he says. "I like wires."

Harry laughs. "I'm surprised you had a job in your prior life," he says. "That's more than you can say this time around."

Holliston glares at him again.

"What's the offer?" I ask them both.

"What's the difference?" Holliston demands.

"Humor me," I tell him. "Generally speaking, I try to learn a fact or two about each case before trial begins. Crazy, I know."

"Murder two," Harry says. "Eligible for parole in fifteen. And he'll get it if he keeps his hands clean and his mouth zipped."

"You can't *not* consider it," I tell Holliston.

He turns toward me, his eyes wild, apparently infuriated by my audacity. "You don't know a goddamn thing about it," he says.

"You're wrong there," I tell him, meeting his angry eyes. "I know a few things. I know you're looking at life if you get bagged for murder one, for instance. I know life means life, as in, until you draw your last breath behind bars. And I know this deal gets you out in your late thirties—still young enough to build a decent future. Only a complete fool would reject it out of hand."

Holliston snorts and spreads his arms wide, as if he's onstage and the house is sold out. "What's with you people?" he asks. "First I get this guy"—he tosses his head toward Harry—"wantin' to sell me down the river. And now you come in here tellin' me I don't need to have a life till fifteen years from now. What the hell kind of sorry lawyers are you? Ever hear of stickin' up for your client, for Chrissake?"

"Advising you is part of our job," Harry tries again.

"And you already done that part," Holliston fires back. "I ain't takin' your advice. And I'm the boss here. So give it a rest. Get to the other part of your job. Tellin' me how to tell them people what happened that night. I want it done right. I want everything crystal clear. And I don't want nothin' left out."

Harry drums his fingers on the table and his eyes move to mine. He's resigned. Holliston is correct; at this particular point in the process, he *is* the boss. He claims he acted only as necessary to preserve his own life. If the jury believes him, he'll walk away a free man. And like it or not, we have a duty to try to make that happen.

Harry stops drumming and again leans back on the two rear legs of his chair, staring at Holliston. He cups his hands behind his head, fingers laced, elbows akimbo, and takes a deep breath. "Go ahead," he says to our system-savvy client at last. "Tell us your tale."

CHAPTER 4

My son is a freshman at Boston College. He finished first-semester finals on Friday and he's home now for winter break. I'm surprised to see his pickup in the driveway of our Windmill Lane cottage, though, when Harry and I pull up at six o'clock. I thought Luke would be out with his buddies by now, cruising Main Street or shooting pool at the Piping Plover Pub.

Harry and I hang our damp coats on hooks inside the kitchen door before we wander into the living room. The woodstove is crackling and the TV is on—local news just beginning—but no one's watching. Luke hustles down the stairs and Danny Boy, our twelve-year-old Irish setter, saunters behind, his tail wagging instantly at the sight of his buddy Harry. "Mom," Luke says as his six-foot-three frame stoops in front of the mirror above the couch, "I'm really glad you're here."

This sentiment can mean only one thing: my son is broke.

"Could you float me some cash?" he asks, running one hand through the thin black locks he inherited from me. "I'll pay you back when I'm working."

"And when will that be?" I know the answer, of course. No time soon. Long after this loan and dozens of others have faded from memory.

He tugs at his chin, struggling to figure out the answer to my perplexing question. "Summer," he says. "I'll pay you back in the summer."

If I didn't know better, I'd think he was serious. I find a twenty in my jacket pocket and hand it to him.

He winces.

"What?" I ask. "You need more?"

"Maybe another?" he says, his voice pleading.

"Another what?"

"Another twenty?" He squints when he says this, almost closing his eyes against his own request.

"You need forty bucks?"

"I have a date," he says, "and I want to take her someplace decent."

Harry pulls his tattered wallet from his back pants pocket and presses a second twenty into Luke's palm. "I'll contribute," Harry says. "Young love is one of my favorite causes."

I expect Luke to balk at the mention of love, but he doesn't. "Hey, thanks," he says instead, punching Harry on the arm. "I'm good for it. Honest."

Harry flops down in the middle of the couch, props his feet on the coffee table, and spreads his arms out across the top cushions. Danny Boy hops up and sits beside him, then curls into a big ball and rests his graying head on Harry's lap. They both watch Luke stoop again to double-check his hair in the mirror. "Who is she?" Harry laughs, scratching Danny Boy's ears. "Who's the lucky lass?"

"You won't believe it," Luke says, grabbing his parka from the closet under the stairs. "She's the Senator's daughter. And she's great."

I freeze. "Which senator?"

"Kendrick," he answers, zipping his coat. "Abby Kendrick. I just met her a few days ago."

"How'd *that* happen?" Senator Kendrick and his wife have only one child. And everyone in the Commonwealth knows she's following her father's footsteps through the hallowed halls of Harvard. She's a sophomore this year.

Luke shrugs. "Her roommate is dating a guy in my dorm," he says. "And they finished with finals an entire week before we did. A week and a day," he adds, as if the extra day is what really frosts him. "They finished last Thursday." He shakes his head. "Last Thursday," he repeats, certain Harry and I would be sobbing by now if we'd heard him the first time.

"Anyway, they came over to visit the night they finished and a bunch of us went out for Thai to celebrate, I guess. Course, the girls were the only ones who had anything to celebrate then. They went home after dinner; we went back to the dorm to study for more crummy exams. But Abby and I ended up sitting next to each other at the Thai place, and we got to talking. She's staying in town with her folks—they have a summer place on Old Harbor Road—through the holidays. So I asked if she'd like to grab a bite sometime and she said *sure*." He turns to Harry. "Can you believe it? She said *sure*."

Harry kicks his shoes off and loosens his tie. "Life is good," he tells Danny Boy, "whenever she says *sure*."

"Hey, look at that," Luke says. "There she is."

For a split second, I think Abby must have come to our door. Luke's eyes don't move in that direction, though. He's staring at the TV. And there she is.

Senator Kendrick is on-screen, flanked by his wife and daughter. His lips are moving, but it's not his words we hear. Instead, a talking head in the upper right corner tells us the Senator held a press conference outside his Chatham home at four o'clock today. He repeated the detailed descriptions we've been hearing on the news all day—of Michelle Forrester, her electric-blue BMW roadster, and the clothes she was wearing when she was last seen four days ago. He pleaded for anyone with information about her—no matter how insignificant it might seem—to come forward. He also gave out a newly established 800 number for his D.C. office. His staff, he said, would gladly accept calls from persons not willing to contact the police directly.

So much for my *keep your mouth shut* admonition. Harry's right. My newest client isn't very good at following directions.

Luke zips up his parka, then walks closer to the TV screen and points at the Senator's daughter. "Is she great," he says, turning back to face Harry and me, "or what?"

My son is right. Abby Kendrick is tall and lean—athletic-looking—with dark red hair, an alabaster complexion, and finely carved features like her father's. She's perfectly poised in front of the cameras. And she's stunning.

Harry lets out a low whistle as he gets up from the couch and pulls two more twenties from his wallet. "Take her someplace better than decent," he says, handing the folded bills to Luke. "And tell her to order the lobster."

CHAPTER 5

Tuesday, December 14

A grown woman who voluntarily refers to herself as "Honey" is suspect in my book. The Senator's wife has a perfectly serviceable given name—Nell—but she prefers her nectar nickname instead. When she attends her husband's public appearances—campaign stops, fund-raisers, and press conferences—she insists that the members of the media address her by her self-imposed moniker. And now, in her state-of-the-art, sun-drenched kitchen, she demands the same of me. "Please, dear," she says each time I speak to her, "call me Honey." The result, of course, is that I've stopped calling her anything at all.

This is the first time I've met Mrs. Kendrick and I'm not surprised to find her ill at ease, uncomfortable in her own skin. That's exactly how she always seems on television, no matter what the occasion. It took ten minutes to convince her that I really do take my coffee black, that I'm not refusing her repeated offers of cream and sugar out of some misguided sense of propriety. At this rate, the quick chat I'd planned to have with her and her husband this morning will take the rest of the calendar year.

The spacious, all-white kitchen is on the landward side of the house. A rectangular wrought-iron table and six matching, cushioned chairs are situated in an alcove a few feet from glass sliders. The Senator and I are settled across from each other, coffee mugs in hand, my beat-up briefcase on the slate floor beside my chair. We've been here fifteen minutes now, waiting for Honey to join us.

She's an attractive woman, but I suspect she's high-maintenance as well. She's lean like her husband and daughter but not as tall as either of them, with a winter tan and short, salon-assisted amber hair. Honey-colored, I realize as I watch her from across the room. In tailored dark slacks, a powder blue cashmere sweater, and pumps, she looks like she thinks I came here this morning to take photos. It's a good thing I didn't; Honey seems constitutionally unable to stop moving. She flutters around the room, opening and closing drawers and cupboards; stacking and restacking newspapers and magazines on the counter; offering us coffee cake, fruit, and yogurt.

"Not for me," I tell her a third time. Her husband says no again too, then stares through the sliders to the snow-covered yard and the neighboring bungalow. Mrs. Kendrick turns her back to us, roots through the supersize, stainless steel refrigerator, and delivers a fruit salad and three vanilla yogurts to the table anyway. "Honey," the Senator says quietly, "please join us. Marty doesn't have all day."

He's right about that. I'm supposed to meet Harry at the House

26

of Correction at ten—an hour from now—and it's a forty-minute drive from here. Today we'll do our best to prepare Derrick Holliston for cross-examination. And though it's impossible to know how cross will go for any client—or any witness, for that matter—with Holliston we know one thing for sure: it'll get ugly.

Mrs. Kendrick nods at her husband's request and wipes her hands on a terry-cloth towel. She doesn't sit, though. She leans against one slider, wrings the red-checkered towel, and turns her attention to me. I'd better get to the point, I guess. She doesn't look like she plans to stand still for long.

"You need to be quiet," I tell them both.

"What?" the Senator says.

There's no doubt in my mind that he heard me. He just can't wrap his brain around the message. "About Michelle Forrester," I add. "You need to zip it, publicly and privately. No more press conferences. No more media events of any kind. No more conversation about her, unless it's with me."

The Senator looks into his coffee mug for a moment. When his eyes meet mine again, they're angry. "That's impossible," he says.

"Then you need to find a new attorney."

He sets his mug down, hard. "Are you threatening me?"

"No," I assure him. "But I am telling you I'm a defense lawyer, not a magician. I can't protect your interests if you can't keep your mouth shut."

"You're being unreasonable," he says. "That young woman worked for me every day for the past three and a half years and she's vanished without a trace. You expect me to stand by and say nothing?"

"That's right. Until we get a handle on what's happened here, that's exactly what I expect."

He looks into his mug again, silent for now. I turn to his wife. She shifts away from me, leans sideways, the towel still taut between her clenched hands. Her shoulder presses against the glass and her gaze settles on the shingled bungalow next door. "And I expect it from both of you," I tell her.

She doesn't react at first, as if she's receiving my words via satellite. "Me?" she says at last. "What in the world do I have to do with it?"

"Plenty. At this point, anyone who ever crossed paths with Michelle Forrester has something to do with it."

Honey looks over at her husband and gives him a tight, decidedly unsweetened smile. He doesn't look back at her, though; he's still staring into his mug. "Well," she says, "Michelle and I certainly crossed *paths*."

I intend to find out what she means by that, but quick footsteps on the stairs in the next room make me hold my tongue. Abby Kendrick breezes into the kitchen in gray sweats and white sneakers, her long, lustrous hair in a loose ponytail. She pours a tall glass of orange juice from the ceramic pitcher on the counter before she looks up at any of us. Her pale, gray-blue eyes match her father's; they widen as she takes her first sip. "Oh," she says, "sorry. I didn't know we had company."

"Abby"—her father lifts his coffee mug toward me—"this is Ms. Nickerson."

She gives me a little wave from across the room.

"Call me Marty," I say, hoping I don't sound too much like Honey.

She nods, studying me as she takes another swallow. Her expression says she's certain she knows me from somewhere but can't quite put her finger on it.

I know how she recognizes me, of course, and I wonder if Abby needs her gorgeous gray-blues examined. Aside from our nine-inch height difference, Luke and I are dead ringers for each other. We share the same black hair, fair skin, and dark blue eyes. She realizes before I say anything, though. "You're Luke Ellis's mom, aren't you?" she says. "God, you look just like him."

I nod, swallowing the urge to point out that it's actually the other way around.

"I had dinner with him last night," she tells me.

"So I heard. He managed to squeeze me in for five minutes before he dashed out to pick you up." I have no idea what Luke would've wanted me to say in response to Abby's comment, but I'm pretty sure that wasn't it.

She raises one eyebrow. "You're a lawyer, aren't you?"

I nod again, amazed. My son must have mentioned his mother.

She sets her glass on the counter, looks from one parent to the other, then frowns. "Why are the two of you talking to a lawyer?"

Her mother walks toward her—and away from our discussion—before the question ends. "It doesn't concern you, Abigail."

Abby stares at her father, her eyes saying she fully expects an answer. He hesitates for a moment, watching his wife's back, then meets his daughter's gaze. "We're discussing the Forrester matter," he says.

"What about it?" This time the question is directed at me, but the Senator answers first. "We're talking about the investigation," he says. "That's all."

Abby folds her arms and smirks. "Investigation? Please. No need for an investigation. I know exactly what happened." She stares angrily at her father. "And so do you."

"Abigail," her mother snaps, "this isn't the time."

"Too much nose candy." Abby fires her words at me, ignoring her mother. "That's what happened. Too much white stuff up the nose."

Silence. For a moment, no one in the room seems to breathe. Even the perpetually mobile Honey is paralyzed.

Finally, the Senator takes a deep breath and turns to me. "Michelle had a problem," he says, "a couple of years back. But she was past that. She'd put it behind her."

"Oh, right." Abby laughs, but it's not a happy one. She takes her half-empty glass of juice from the counter and heads out of the kitchen. "Sure she did," she calls over her shoulder, her ponytail bobbing. "And she gave up *men* too. The word on the street is she was headed straight for the convent."

Honey scowls at her husband, slaps her twisted towel on the counter and follows her daughter toward the living room. She pauses, though, in the doorway, and turns back to me. "I'll be happy to abide by your instructions," she says. "As far as I'm concerned, the name Michelle Forrester need never be mentioned again."

Senator Kendrick plants his elbows on the table and buries his face in his hands as his wife leaves the kitchen. I set down my coffee mug, check my watch, and wait. I had two appointments scheduled for this morning. This was supposed to be the easy one.

CHAPTER 6

Derrick Holliston has had a change of heart, it seems. I'm only about twenty minutes late for our jailhouse meeting, but apparently he and Harry have already covered a lot of ground. "Maybe I won't, then," he says as the young guard with the crew cut pulls the meeting room door shut behind me. "Maybe I won't."

"Won't what?" I already know the answer, I think—his tone tells me more than his words—but I want to be sure.

"Testify," Holliston says as I join him and Harry at the rickety table. "Maybe I'll just keep my mouth shut."

I'm a little concerned about what led to this switch. I'm no fan of Holliston's—Harry's instincts about him are dead-on, I'm certain—but like it or not, he *is* our client. If he wants to take the witness stand—and he sure as hell did yesterday—it's not our job to talk him out of it. "Hold on," I tell him as I turn toward Harry. "Fill me in."

"We were just going over the police report," Harry says, tossing his pen on top of a dog-eared copy of it. "It's in there. The whole *story*." His emphasis on the last word says it all. It's a fairy tale, as far as he's concerned. A grim one.

"So?" I ask. I'm pretty sure I know where this is going, though.

"So Tommy Fitzpatrick will say it for us," Harry answers. "The Chief questioned Holliston personally, as soon as he was picked up, and recorded his version of events. My bet is Fitzpatrick will be the Commonwealth's first witness. He prepared the primary report and he'll testify to its content. All of it."

Holliston not only waived his right to remain silent on the morning of his arrest, he spilled his guts to anyone—and everyone—who'd listen. While that's generally not a good idea, it just might work to his advantage now. His story has been memorialized at least a half dozen times, once in painstaking detail by Tommy Fitzpatrick, Chatham's Chief of Police.

"So the jurors will hear what happened," Holliston explains, as though he's my lawyer, "but they don't hear nothin' about my priors."

His priors aren't pretty. If the prosecutor were to line them up side by side, in chronological order, the jury would see the perfect evolution of a sociopath, each crime more violent than its predecessor. The jury won't see anything of the sort, though, because the prosecutor can't do that—Holliston committed all but one of his crimes when he was under eighteen.

"Most of your priors won't come in anyhow," I remind him. "Your juvenile record is sealed."

"Yeah, but I got that assault." He sighs. "That'll come in. And it don't make me look good." He shakes his head slowly, his lips tight, his eyes saying it's a damned shame the world dealt him that blow.

Holliston has only one conviction on his adult tab, an accomplishment made possible by the fact that he's spent all but five weeks of his over-eighteen life in jail. If he takes the stand in this trial, that conviction will come in. It's a given. And it's a problem.

Four years ago, the manager of one of Chatham's premier restaurants was assaulted and robbed. Bobby "the Butcher" Frazier, longtime caretaker of Kristen's Pub, was closing the place that February night, the off-season regulars and a handful of employees out the door just minutes ahead of him. As he stood on the snowy brick walkway inserting his key to flip the back door's deadlock, a young white male wearing a ski mask emerged from the darkness of the parking lot. He demanded the night deposit sack Bobby had stashed under one arm.

The Butcher isn't a guy who takes kindly to bullies. He told the masked man to take a hike. A fistfight ensued and Bobby was stabbed during the course of it, the knife penetrating just below his right shoulder. Down but not out, he grabbed his attacker's hand—along with the knife inside it—and continued to fight. Eventually, though, the masked man kicked Bobby to the ground and fled with the cash.

The Butcher was lucky; his injuries weren't all that serious. He was treated at Cape Cod Hospital that night and released the next day, but because of his assailant's mask he was unable to give the police a description beyond approximate height and weight. The Chatham cops suspected Derrick Holliston from the start—he'd been released from a juvenile detention facility just a few days earlier, on his eighteenth birthday—but they had precious little in the way of evidence to back up their suspicions. Until they got the results from the Commonwealth's crime lab.

DNA evidence pegged him. Holliston must have sustained a substantial cut during his struggle with the Butcher. Blood evidence tied him to the scene, to the victim, and eventually, to the empty cash sack retrieved from a town-owned Dumpster a block from the pub. The knife was never found, but the ski mask was, and hair follicles hammered yet another nail into his coffin. On top of all that, the unemployed Holliston had more than two grand in cash when he was arrested at the Monomoy Moorings Motel. Even so, Holliston and the unfortunate lawyer appointed to defend him relied upon what Harry calls the SODDI defense: Some Other Dude Did It.

The jury didn't think so. The judge sentenced Holliston to five-to-seven and with time off for good behavior—he was a model prisoner, according to his discharge papers—he served just over four. He'd been out little more than a month when Father McMahon was murdered—stabbed and left bleeding on the sacristy floor—and St. Veronica's Christmas Eve collection disappeared.

"Yeah," Holliston says, pointing at Harry, "for once you're right. We'll let Fitzpatrick do it. I kinda like the idea of the Police Chief tellin' them what happened. Gives it a little . . . what's the word?"

"Credibility?" I ask.

He snaps his fingers. "That's it. Credibility. I like that."

Harry closes his eyes, shakes his head.

"You have the cop tell it," Holliston says.

"Not me," Harry answers, pointing in my direction. "Marty's taking the Chief. And don't worry, she'll get the whole story from him."

Holliston looks at me and half laughs. "Even better," he says. "So it's settled. I ain't takin' the stand."

"Hold on," I tell him for the second time in ten minutes. "This is an important decision. Don't rush it."

He shrugs. "The top cop tells the jurors what I told him and as far as they know, I'm an altar boy. What do I got to lose?"

He *does* have something to lose—something important. And his defense attorneys need to tell him so.

I look across the table and Harry arches his eyebrows. It's my turn, I guess. "Look," I tell Holliston, "don't get me wrong. All things considered, I think you're making the right decision. But don't underestimate the impact your silence will have on the panel. Jurors like to hear from defendants."

"But if I take the stand"—he tugs at his stubbled chin—"they hear about that other guy, too, the Butcher."

He's right about that. If he testifies that he stabbed the priest only to save his own life, the prosecutor will be entitled to introduce his prior conviction—for stabbing a man in order to rob him. "Like I said," I tell him, "on balance I think keeping your mouth shut makes sense. I just want to be sure you're aware of the downside."

"Okay," he says. "I get it. I still ain't takin' the stand."

Harry shuts his file and starts repacking his battered schoolbag. "Well," he says, not looking at Holliston, "then we'll see you in the morning. If you're not taking the stand, there's no need to prepare you for cross."

Holliston smiles at Harry, then at me. "Right again," he says to Harry. "You're on a roll."

Harry ignores him, bangs on the door for the guard.

Holliston's still smiling as he leaves. "Go ahead," he says over his shoulder. "Take the rest of the day off. Both of you."

CHAPTER 7

Taking the rest of the day off isn't an option for either of us. Harry went straight back to the office when we left the county complex, to spend the rest of the day—and probably most of the evening—preparing for trial. I took the Mid-Cape Highway in the opposite direction, destination Stamford. For reasons I can't articulate—not even to myself—I want to meet the Forresters. Maybe I want to get some sense of Michelle through her family, to find out if she might have chosen to disappear for a while, to glean some idea of where she might have gone if the worst hasn't happened. Whatever the reason, my gut tells me to do it now, not later.

Michelle's mother was hesitant when I called from the road. No doubt Geraldine Schilling advised the family to speak only with representatives of law enforcement, whether from the Commonwealth or the State of Connecticut. After a few minutes of conversation, though, Mrs. Forrester relented. She muffled her telephone's mouthpiece, consulted with her husband in hushed tones, and then agreed they'd meet with me at their home this afternoon. I was pretty confident they would. Generally speaking, parents of missing people will talk with just about anyone.

Traffic is light—no surprise in the middle of a snow-blown weekday—and I find myself pulling into the Forresters' gravel driveway a little past three, less than four hours after leaving Barnstable. I park my tired Thunderbird next to a blue Jaguar, shiny beneath a thin coat of fresh snow, in front of a buttoned-up, two-car garage. I'm not the only visitor, it seems. I grab my briefcase and walk back toward the Forresters' front entrance, wondering what in the world I'll have to say when I get there.

Their colonial is large, though not as imposing as other houses I passed on this block, with cream-colored clapboards and hunter green shutters. Dormant rosebushes ramble along the sides of the house and into the spacious backyard, tented with multiple layers of straw-colored burlap. A full-size, in-ground swimming pool is sealed for the season, dead leaves scattered across its blue vinyl surface. And a screened deck above the pool, off the back of the house, is elegantly furnished for al fresco dining.

The front door is already open when I reach the short flight of wooden steps leading to the porch. "Attorney Nickerson?" A woman in jeans and a black turtleneck hurries outside, not stopping for a coat.

"Marty," I tell her, extending my hand. She's about thirty, obviously not Michelle Forrester's mother. The sister, I realize after a moment; she's the older sister who spoke briefly with TV reporters last night. She's not pretty, exactly, certainly not the way Michelle is. But she's striking in a more subtle, maybe even more interesting way.

"Meredith Forrester," she says as she shakes my hand. "Michelle's sister."

Her shoulder-length hair is jet black like mine, but thicker, more lustrous, like Michelle's. Her complexion is flawless and her pale blue eyes don't quite match; one's a little lighter than the other. "My mother called me at work after she spoke with you," she says. "She asked me to leave a little early and come over; both my parents wanted me to be here for your visit. I hope you don't mind."

"Not a bit," I assure her.

"I want to mention something to you," she says, folding her arms at her waist, "before we go inside."

"Meredith, you'll catch your death of pneumonia! Why in the world won't you girls wear coats?" It's Michelle—thirty-five years from now. She's in the doorway, frantically waving at both of us, telling us to come in from the cold.

"This is my mother," Meredith says as we enter. "Catherine."

I shake Catherine's hand, then look back at her elder daughter. I want her to hold on to that *before we go inside* thought she wanted to mention. She nods at me; she will. She takes my parka when we enter the foyer and motions for me to follow her mother, who's already into the next room. "Warren," Catherine says, "Mrs. Nickerson is here. The lawyer who called earlier."

Warren is on his feet when I enter the living room, in front of a brown leather recliner, his cardigan unbuttoned and his pipe unlit. He turns my way and I realize he's the source of Meredith's slightly mismatched eyes. He looks older than his sixty years; no doubt he's aged a decade in the past few days. His handshake is firm, his lined face exhausted. I've seen this haunted look before—more than a few times—but I'll never get used to it.

"Call me Marty," I tell him.

"Marty it is," he says. His words are flat, without inflection. He points the stem of his pipe at a small sofa. "Please," he says, "have a seat."

"Can I get you anything?" Catherine asks. "A cup of tea, maybe?"

I shake my head as I settle on one end of the sofa, next to the welcome warmth of a crackling fire. The last thing Catherine Forrester needs foisted on her now is hostess duty. "Thank you, but no," I tell her. "I'll only stay a few minutes; I won't take too much of your time."

Warren lets out a halfhearted laugh. "Time," he says, still cradling the bowl of his pipe. "We've got plenty of that."

Meredith crosses the room and sits beside me while her mother claims the chair next to Warren's, a smaller, upholstered version of his. Their side-by-side recliners haven't been new in a long time, but they've aged gracefully.

"Catherine tried to explain," Warren says, his brow knitting, "but I'm still not clear. What is your role in this . . . situation?" He looks down at his pipe, as if the answer might be tamped inside its bowl.

"I represent Senator Kendrick," I tell him.

"Why?" he says.

Fair question. "Because the authorities have been talking with him. And that's entirely appropriate; they should. But anyone being interrogated in a serious investigation is well advised to be represented by counsel."

He nods, but the furrows in his forehead deepen. My explanation doesn't make sense to him, but he's too polite to say so. "We watched the Senator's press conference yesterday," he says instead. "We appreciate everything he's doing. Tell him that for us, will you?"

A guilt spasm seizes my stomach. Just a few hours ago, I put the kibosh on any future press conferences; I don't mention that, though. "I will," I assure the weary Warren Forrester. "I'll tell him."

"That number," Catherine says, "that eight-hundred number Senator Kendrick gave out, I think that's going to help; I think it will make a real difference. Someone is bound to call in, someone who's seen Michelle."

Catherine's voice cracks when she says her younger daughter's name, but she nods emphatically at each of us, dry-eyed. She means what she just said; she believes it. Hope is a relentless emotion.

"Is it possible," I ask, "that Michelle simply needed some time away? Felt overwhelmed by the pressures of her high-profile job and decided to escape for a while?"

No doubt they've been asked this question—or some version of it—a hundred times. But I have to ask it too; there's no other way I'll hear their answer. The cops aren't in the habit of sharing their files with me. Our District Attorney isn't, either.

"No," Warren says. "That's not possible." Catherine shakes her head. Meredith does too.

"What about college friends?" I ask. "Might she have gone to stay with an old UVA buddy?"

All three shake their heads now. "My parents are sick with worry," Meredith says quietly. "Michelle would never do that to them. Never."

"She wouldn't," Catherine concurs. "That's why we're thinking she may have had an accident. That fancy car of hers is so tiny. And she's always had a lead foot. She could be in a hospital—unidentified—anywhere between here and Hyannis."

She's not, of course. The Massachusetts and Connecticut authorities would have covered that base on day one. I don't say so, though. I don't intend to yank that straw, or any other, from the Forresters' collective grasp. I change the subject instead. "Is there a boyfriend?"

Catherine shakes her head yet again and actually smiles a little. "Boys," she says. "Michelle always has plenty of boys around."

Warren nods in agreement, leans back in his chair, and closes his eyes.

Catherine points toward the kitchen. "Most days that phone rarely rings," she says. "But when Michelle's home—whether for a weekend or a week—it doesn't stop."

"But no one in particular?" I ask. "No one steady?"

"No," Catherine says. "Not that we know of."

Warren nods again, his eyes still closed, and it occurs to me that I'm wearing out my welcome; these people were spent long before I showed up. And besides, I'm hoping Meredith will walk out with me; I'm eager to hear whatever it was she wanted to say earlier.

I stand, take two business cards from my jacket pocket, and hand one to Meredith, the other to her mother. "I won't keep you any longer. But please call if you think of anything—anything at all—we might have overlooked. Senator Kendrick will do everything he can to help."

Warren's eyes open at the mention of the Senator's name. "Don't forget to thank him for us," he says as he stands.

"I won't," I assure him.

Meredith gets to her feet as I say my good-byes to her parents. "I'll see you out," she says as she walks toward the kitchen ahead of me.

"Wear a coat," Catherine calls after us.

Meredith is quiet as she hands me my parka and then dutifully dons her heavy black overcoat. We exit into the late afternoon cold and she pauses on the porch, at the top of the steps. "There is something else," she says. "It's what I wanted to tell you when you first got here. I don't think it matters, really, but since you're the Senator's attorney, I guess it's okay to mention it to you. Maybe you already know."

I stop one step below her and shrug, hoping to give the impression that I probably *do* already know. But I'm pretty sure I don't.

"My sister is in love with Charles Kendrick," she says, fingering her top button. "And I believe he loves her, too."

This news isn't exactly a shock. Honey's performance this morning gave me a pretty good push in that direction. Still, I'm grateful to have my hunch confirmed. Maybe that's why I came here in the first place.

"They had an affair," Meredith continues. "They started seeing each other—secretly—after she'd worked for him a couple of years. He ended it four months ago, when his wife found out."

I nod.

"Michelle was distraught," she says. "I went to D.C. and spent a few days with her right after it all fell apart. She was devastated, couldn't even go into the office that week."

I nod again, thinking I need to have yet another heart-to-heart with my not-so-candid client.

"I know it sounds tawdry," Meredith says as she starts down the steps, "but it wasn't. I only saw them together a few times, but there was no denying they had genuine feelings for each other. The air between them was electric."

I study Meredith for a moment, wondering if she's angry with the Senator for hurting her little sister. If she is, it doesn't show. I decide not to ask. "Do your parents know?" I say instead.

She takes a deep breath. "At some level they do," she says, "but they'd never admit it. They wouldn't approve."

"Meredith." I stand still in the middle of the snowy driveway and she does too. "You're under no obligation to tell me anything. But I'd really like to know if you've mentioned this to anyone else."

She looks down at her boots. "The District Attorney," she says. "Ms. Schilling."

"Geraldine."

She nods. "Honestly, I wasn't trying to cause trouble for him—politically or personally. That's the last thing Michelle would want me to do. But I couldn't *not* mention it. What if it turned out to matter somehow and I had kept quiet?"

She's not crying, but her eyes are filled to the brim. "You did the right thing," I tell her. "And I appreciate your answering my question."

She shakes my hand, then turns and heads back to her parents' house.

It's barely four o'clock when I pull out of the Forresters' driveway, but the cold December sky is near dark already. I toy with the idea of calling Senator Kendrick from the car, to ask why he insists on keeping his own lawyer in the dark, to ask why he repeatedly enables the District Attorney to stay two steps ahead of me, to ask what other secrets he's keeping. I decide against that call, though. Some conversations should be had face-to-face.

CHAPTER 8

Wednesday, December 15

Judge Richard Gould was elevated from the District Court bench to Superior Court just over a year ago. It was a well-deserved promotion. A highly intelligent, serious man, he runs an efficient, on-schedule courtroom. Even so, any lawyer who's ever practiced before him knows that the procedural and substantive rights of litigants—particularly those of criminal defendants—are his foremost concern. Derrick Holliston is lucky to have ended up on Judge Gould's docket. I told Holliston so before I left the House of Correction yesterday. He promised to send the Governor a thank-you card.

The judge isn't here yet. Neither is Harry. Geraldine Schilling is, though, already set up at the prosecutors' table with her young assistant, Clarence Wexler. They're reviewing exhibits, leaning toward each other from time to time to whisper. They both look relaxed, confident that Holliston's conviction is already in the bag.

Two court officers bustle about behind us, seating sixty potential jurors in the old courtroom's small but stately gallery. The men and women are silent as they file in, winter coats folded over their arms. Their eyes are alert, their faces somber. From them, Geraldine and Harry will select fourteen, twelve of whom will decide Derrick Holliston's fate.

The side door opens and a prison guard enters, heavy holster low on his hips. Our client follows and a second guard—a near-clone of the first—brings up the rear, completing the Holliston sandwich. The accused is free of hardware, wearing black slacks, a dark gray suit coat, and a white dress shirt, neatly pressed. I'm taken aback.

All criminal defendants are permitted to "clean up" for trial— get a haircut, a shave, a set of decent street clothes—but this particular defendant cleans up exceptionally well. His once greasy brown hair has been recently introduced to shampoo. It's trimmed short and parted precisely. The sketchy mustache is gone, as is every other trace of facial hair. His near-constant sneer has been erased. He looks like the guy next door—if the guy next door happens to be an Eagle Scout.

A low murmur emanates from the crowded gallery as Holliston approaches the defense table, his expression blank. He settles into the seat next to mine—the one farthest from the bench—without looking at me. "Get rid of the cat-licks," he says matter-of-factly.

It takes a moment for me to get it. "We don't know their religions," I tell him. "The jury questionnaire doesn't ask that."

He snorts and the familiar sneer resurfaces. "What?" he says, his voice low. "You don't know one when you see one?"

"I guess not."

He shakes his head at my incompetence. "That lady there"—he twists in his chair toward the benches behind us and the sneer evaporates again—"on the end, front row. She look like a cat-lick to you?"

"She looks Italian," I answer.

He faces front and plants both hands on the table, resting his case. "You ever knowed a guinea what *ain't* a cat-lick?"

I lean back against the worn leather of the high-backed chair and close my eyes. Some conversations aren't worth finishing.

Harry arrives, pulls out the chair on the other side of mine, and hoists his bulging schoolbag onto the defense table. He doesn't sit, though. "What's up?" he asks, snapping open the bag's metal clasp.

"We were discussing the finer points of jury selection," I tell him.

He glances sideways at me as he unpacks, then blinks twice when he takes in our client's new persona.

"So what's the plan here?" Holliston says from my other side. "You people got a plan or you just wingin' it?"

Harry laughs and tosses the pleadings file, a blank legal pad, and a few pens on the table. He says nothing.

"Judge Gould likes to complete jury selection the first morning," I tell our client. "And he usually does. It'll be a late lunch break, though."

Holliston purses his lips; he seems not to approve of late lunches.

"After that," I continue, "the prosecuting attorney will deliver her opening statement. If there's time, Harry will deliver his before we wrap up for the day."

"And if there ain't time?"

I shrug. "Then he'll do it tomorrow morning. Either way, he'll open. Don't worry."

"Oh, I'm worried," Holliston says, staring up at Harry. "I got good reason to worry."

Harry doesn't let on he hears. He walks away from us, delivers a short stack of documents to Geraldine, another to the courtroom clerk. Judge Gould emerges from chambers as Harry returns to our table. Billy "Big Red" O'Reilly tells us to rise.

"What the hell is that?" Holliston mutters, his eyes on Big Red.

"He's the bailiff," I whisper back. Holliston knows a fair number of the courthouse players, no doubt, but he's probably never laid eyes on O'Reilly. Big Red is the seniormost bailiff in the county complex and, as he's fond of reminding those with less seniority, he doesn't work kiddie court. It's dress rehearsal.

"We need a new one," Holliston informs me as the judge sits and tells everyone in the room to do likewise.

"A new what?" The words escape before I can stop them. I'm a little slow on the uptake this morning, but I don't really need an answer to that question.

I get one anyhow. "A new bailiff," Holliston says. "I don't want no mick hangin' around my jury."

I turn in my chair so I can look him in the eyes. "Funny thing. You don't get to choose your bailiff. The Bill of Rights doesn't stretch that far." He opens his mouth to argue, but I beat him to the punch. "Shut up," I tell him. "A trial's about to start here."

Oddly enough, he obeys.

Judge Gould has already welcomed the sixty citizens seated in the gallery. He thanks them for their willingness to serve, then gestures to those of us seated at the tables. All four lawyers stand and face the back of the courtroom. After a signal from me, Holliston does too. Sans sneer.

"Ladies and gentlemen," the judge says, "before we get started,

I'd like all of you to look at the lawyers and the defendant involved in this case. If you even think you might know any of them—no matter how remotely—please raise your hand."

Four go up.

"You, sir." The judge points to an elderly gentleman in the front row. He's wearing his Sunday best, right down to the perfectly pressed triangle of white handkerchief protruding from his jacket pocket. "Which of them do you know?" Judge Gould asks.

The older man stands, points his hat at Geraldine. "The District Attorney," he says. "She's a neighbor."

"Thank you for telling us. You're dismissed with the sincere gratitude of the court." The judge nods to the two officers standing against the back wall and one hustles down the center aisle to usher the disqualified juror out of the courtroom.

The elderly gentleman looks surprised at first, then nods and dutifully follows the uniform toward the back doors. This won't necessarily end his jury service. He may find himself downstairs in one of the smaller courtrooms before the day is out, on a civil panel. If our DA is his neighbor, defense lawyers will bounce him from all criminal proceedings, even if Geraldine isn't in the room.

"And you, ma'am?" Judge Gould directs his question to a middle-aged woman six rows back. She points to Geraldine too. "I don't *really* know her," she says, looking a little embarrassed. "I've just seen her on the news."

Most of them have seen all of us on the news, of course. But it's Geraldine they remember. Always.

"You may be seated," Judge Gould says. He looks out at the whole panel. "We're not concerned at the moment about anything you might have seen or heard through the media. We want to know about personal contact, if any."

A young man who looks not much older than Luke stands in the row behind the woman who just sat down. "Same here," he says, gesturing toward her. "I just know the lawyers from TV. All of them, I think."

"That's fine," the judge answers.

The final hand-raiser gets to his feet in the back row and the four attorneys laugh. Judge Gould does too. "Mr. Saunders," he says, leaning back in his tall leather chair, "I guess it's safe to say you know everyone up here."

Bert Saunders has been practicing law in Barnstable County since I was in high school. "Four out of five," he says to the judge. "Haven't met the defendant."

"Well, you may as well head back to your office," Judge Gould tells him. "I'm sure you've got plenty of work waiting. And we all know you're not going to serve on this panel—or any other, for that matter."

He's right. Lawyers don't let lawyers serve on juries. It's too risky. A lawyer-juror would almost certainly have an undue influence on the others—even if unintentional. And given that Bert has spent his entire career with the criminal defense bar, no prosecutor in the country would allow him to serve on a capital case. Geraldine would sooner seat the defendant's mother in the jury box.

Bert bends to retrieve his briefcase, then smooths his suit coat and gives us a small salute before heading for the doors.

"Who's the fat guy?" Holliston asks as we reclaim our chairs.

I wonder if he has an adjective in his vocabulary that isn't derogatory. "Bert Saunders is one of the best criminal defense lawyers in the county," I tell him.

Holliston frowns, looking past me to Harry. "Too bad. I could use one of them."

"Ladies and gentlemen," the judge says, "I'm going to read a brief description of the case we're about to try. When I finish, I will ask each of you to consider whether anything you've heard will make it particularly difficult for you to be fair and impartial. I caution you that nothing I say constitutes evidence. What I am about to read is merely a summary of the positions taken by each side."

It's far more than that. Geraldine and Harry have been battling for weeks over the content of the short passage the jury is about to hear. Every word a judge utters during a murder trial is taken to heart by jurors. They have a difficult job, to say the least; they look for guidance wherever they can. And when the judge is as obviously fair-minded as Richard Gould, his summary of the case may well end up being theirs.

"Last Christmas Eve," the judge reads, adjusting his dark-framed glasses, "Francis Patrick McMahon, a Roman Catholic priest assigned to St. Veronica's Parish in Chatham, was found dead on the floor of the chapel's sacristy. The collection money from the seven o'clock Christmas Vigil Mass was gone. The Medical Examiner determined that the deceased had suffered multiple puncture wounds, one of which proved fatal. The Commonwealth accuses the defendant of inflicting those wounds. It charges him with first-degree murder, committed with extreme atrocity or cruelty."

Judge Gould pauses for a sip of water. The citizens seated in the gallery are silent, paralyzed. Even those of us at the tables are frozen.

"The accused, Derrick John Holliston, does not deny inflicting the fatal wound," the judge continues. "But he does dispute the allegation that his actions constitute murder. He maintains that his conduct on the night in question was entirely lawful, that the deceased was the assailant. More specifically, the defendant maintains that the deceased became sexually aggressive and when he—the defendant—resisted, the deceased became violent. The defendant contends that he acted only as necessary to preserve his own life."

Judge Gould pauses again. Still, not a sound. Not a breath, even. "The Commonwealth disputes the defendant's self-defense claim. And the cash from the Christmas Vigil Mass collection has not been recovered."

This final piece of information is more significant than the potential jurors know. Had the police been able to locate the missing money and tie it to Holliston, Geraldine would have charged him pursuant to the felony-murder rule. And she would much rather have done so. Under that rule, a person who causes the death of another while in the process of committing a felony is automatically guilty of first-degree murder, even if the death was unintended. If the rule could be successfully invoked, Geraldine's burden would be substantially lightened: no need to prove premeditation; no need to prove intent, and no need to show extreme atrocity or cruelty.

As it stands, though, the Christmas Eve collection is nowhere to be found. Without it, the underlying felony can't even be charged, let alone proved. As long as the money is missing, the felony-murder rule doesn't come into play. And if the jurors buy Holliston's self-defense claim—if they believe he had to stab the priest in order to save his own life—he'll walk.

The judge removes his glasses, sets them on the bench, and leans on his forearms. "I ask each of you to take a moment now," he says to the assembly, "and reflect. This will not be an easy case for anyone involved. The evidence from both sides will be graphic, detailed. It will be difficult to see and hear; that's a given. But I ask each of you to alert us now if you believe you will have particular trouble being fair and impartial, looking at all of the exhibits and listening to all of the testimony with an open mind."

We attorneys swivel our chairs so we can see the jurors seated behind us. Holliston doesn't move. For a moment, the silence blanketing the courtroom remains undisturbed. But then a man in an end seat in the center of the room gets to his feet and steps into the aisle. He looks to be about fifty, wearing blue jeans, a flannel shirt, and work boots. "I might have a problem with that," he says.

Two well-dressed women follow his lead. The first moves into the aisle across from him. She's about my age, in a tailored, navy blue pants suit and heels. "I may also," she says. The second woman is probably seventy. She stands in the middle of the back row, her silver hair styled and stiff above the collar of a charcoal gray coatdress. She nods at the judge but says nothing, a silent *ditto*.

"Thank you," Judge Gould says to all of them. "Thank you for your candor. Now I ask the three of you to come forward."

They hesitate. They weren't expecting this. It's routine, though. Judge Gould will question each of them individually, in the privacy of his chambers. If a potential juror *does* have a partiality problem, the last thing the judge wants to do is share it with the others.

Dottie Bearse has been Judge Gould's courtroom clerk since his District Court days. When he made the move to Superior Court, he arranged for her to transfer as well. I've never heard the judge ask her for anything; she's always two steps ahead of him. She finishes sorting a stack of papers on her desk now and hands him three juror questionnaires.

"You, sir." The judge consults one of the forms and then looks up at the guy in the work boots. "Mr. Harmon, please take a seat in chambers." Big Red crosses the room and opens the chambers door. All three jurors start down the center aisle.

"And you two"—the judge shifts his attention to the women—"please be seated in the jury box. We'll be with you shortly." The judge stands to leave the bench and Big Red tells the rest of us to rise.

Harry and I head toward chambers, Geraldine and Clarence on our heels. We pause at the door, though, to allow Judge Gould to enter first. He waits too, and directs the jeans-clad juror in ahead of all of us.

The room is small and tidy, lit only by a burnished brass lamp situated on one corner of the judge's dark walnut desk. Judge Gould takes his seat and directs our juror into one of the two chairs facing his. Geraldine settles in the other. Harry leans against a side wall next to the juror, where he can see everyone. Clarence and I hang back by the closed door.

"Mr. Harmon," Judge Gould says, "let me begin by telling you we appreciate your willingness to speak with us. We all do. And let me also assure you, sir, that what you say in this room stays here." The judge glances up at Geraldine, then at Harry. They nod in unison, first at the judge, then at the juror.

"Now what is it, Mr. Harmon, that makes you question your ability to remain impartial?" The judge leans back in his chair, the top of it brushing lightly against the floor-to-ceiling bookcase behind him.

Mr. Harmon looks entirely comfortable, erect in his chair, hands resting on his knees. "Well," he says, clearing his throat, "it's not like I knew the guy or anything."

Geraldine stiffens, her antennae up. The judge fires a cautionary stare her way; he does the questioning in here. "Which guy are we talking about?" he says.

"The priest," Harmon answers. "I went to a Mass he said once. Must've been two years ago now."

We're all quiet for a moment. Anyone with ties to St. Veronica's Parish—religious or otherwise—was weeded out before the sixty juror candidates were brought to the courtroom this morning. Attendance at a single Mass celebrated by the deceased probably didn't show up on the clerk's radar screen.

"I didn't talk to him or anything," Harmon continues. "But he seemed like a decent guy. Didn't seem like somebody who'd . . . well, you know."

"Was this Mass at St. Veronica's?" Judge Gould asks.

Harmon nods.

"How did you happen to be there?"

"My wife's sister lives in that parish," he answers. "She and her husband were celebrating their twenty-fifth wedding anniversary— you know, renewing their vows and all that. Father McMahon said the Mass."

"Was this a private event?" the judge asks.

"Oh no." Mr. Harmon shakes his head. "It was a regular Sunday Mass, but just before the final blessing, he had them come up to the altar to say their *I do*s all over again."

The judge smiles. "And they both did, I presume?"

Mr. Harmon smiles too, first at the judge, then at the rest of us. "Yeah," he says, "they did. And that priest, he made my brother-in-law kiss the 'bride' right there in front of everybody. My wife and I took them out to breakfast afterward and that was all they talked about. They didn't expect to have to do that again."

The judge looks at his hands for a moment, then back up at Harmon. "So you liked Father McMahon?"

"Sure." He shrugs. "When my brother-in-law hesitated—you

know, at the kissing part—the priest led the whole congregation in a big round of applause." Harmon shakes his head, still smiling. "Talk about pressure."

Geraldine is relaxed now, happy even. She wants to keep this juror on the panel. She likes his take on things.

Judge Gould picks up a pen from his desk and taps it in his palm. "Anything else?" he says. "Any other contact with the priest?"

Harmon shakes his head. "Nope. Just saw him that once."

The judge leans forward, sets the pen down again, and clasps his hands together on the desk. "Now Mr. Harmon, clearly you formed a favorable impression of the deceased on that occasion. What we want to know now is whether or not that fact will interfere with your ability to fairly decide this case if you're chosen to serve. Do you believe you're capable of putting your impression from two years ago aside? Will you be able to base your decision strictly on the evidence presented in the courtroom this week?"

Mr. Harmon sits in silence for a moment, considering. I have to give him credit; he thinks about it longer than most. "I believe I can," he says.

"And if the evidence shows that the deceased was, in fact, the aggressor in this case, you would be able to so find?"

Harmon rubs his chin. "If that's what the evidence shows, then yes."

"And if the evidence shows that Mr. Holliston acted only as necessary to preserve his own life, you would vote to acquit?"

Harmon nods, looking thoughtful. "Yes," he says, "I would."

Harry shifts against the wall and faces the desk, but says nothing. He doesn't need to. Judge Gould knows Harry wants to bounce this guy. They'll argue about it later.

"Thank you, sir." The judge stands and motions toward the courtroom. "You may have a seat in the jury box while we speak with the others."

Clarence opens the chambers door and Mr. Harmon exits. Big Red instructs the younger of the two waiting women to join us. Judge Gould checks one of the forms on his desk and smiles at her when she enters. She doesn't smile back.

"Mrs. Meyers," the judge says, "please have a seat." He gives her the same thanks and promise of confidentiality he gave to Mr. Harmon, and then asks her to share her concerns.

She doesn't. She looks down at her lap, then opens her purse and takes a Kleenex from it. I move closer to Harry, so I can see her face. She's blinking back tears. "Please," she says to Judge Gould. "I can't do this. I just can't."

"Take your time," he says quietly, leaning forward on his desk. "When you're ready, tell us why you can't."

We wait while Mrs. Meyers dabs at the corners of her eyes and takes a few deep breaths. "My son," she whispers. She falls silent again.

"What would you like to tell us about him?" The judge's expression is kind, concerned, but Mrs. Meyers doesn't seem to notice. Her small laugh turns at once into a grimace. "Nothing," she says. "I don't *want* to tell you anything about him."

She stares into her lap again and, once more, we wait. "Look," she finally blurts out, "we moved here from St. Bartholomew's."

Everyone in the room reacts. It's as though an invisible hand slapped each of us simultaneously. The judge sits up straighter in his chair. Harry sets his jaw and jams both hands into his pants pockets. Geraldine folds her arms and I find myself doing the same, pressing them hard against my ribs. Even Clarence plants his palms against the wall, looking like he might lose his balance otherwise.

St. Bartholomew's is a parish in the Boston Archdiocese. For eighteen years, it was home to now-defrocked priest Frederick Barlow. A year ago, Barlow admitted to raping twenty-eight boys during his tenure. He's at the Walpole Penitentiary now, doing twelve to fifteen. The twenty-eight boys, of course, are doing life.

After a few moments, Judge Gould recovers. "Was your son involved in the settlement reached last year between the Boston Archdiocese and the Barlow plaintiffs?"

Judges frequently use this device. When speaking with a victim's loved one—especially the parent of a child victim—it's much easier on everyone to refer to the lawsuit or settlement than it is to mention the crimes involved. Even so, Mrs. Meyers flinches at the mention of the former priest's name. "Yes," she says. "My son was one of the plaintiffs. Can we leave it at that?"

"Of course we can," Judge Gould says. "And again, we appreciate your willingness to give us that information."

She twists in her chair and looks toward the door, obviously hoping she can leave now. She can't, though. Not yet.

"Mrs. Meyers," the judge continues.

She faces him again, her eyes wide, surprised. My heart aches for her.

"I have to ask you," he says, "it's my duty to ask this question. Do you believe the information you just shared with us will interfere with your ability to fairly decide this case if you are selected to serve?"

She actually laughs. For the first time since she walked in here, she looks around the room at the rest of us. "Do any of you have children?"

The judge and I both nod.

"What do *you* think?" she asks us.

Judge Gould's eyes meet mine but neither of us speaks. No need.

"Thank you, Mrs. Meyers," the judge says as he stands. "Please return to your seat in the jury box. We'll be done here in a few minutes."

She complies without a word and Big Red sends in the last of our jurors to be interviewed, the silver-haired woman from the back row. "Mrs. Rowlands," the judge says, gesturing toward the empty chair, "please join us."

She does, careful to smooth her coatdress before she sits. Her handbag is the size of a large bread box; it covers her entire lap. "I've had it," she tells us before Judge Gould says another word, "with the entire Roman Catholic Church."

The judge laughs a little, then catches himself. He sits up straighter and forces his face into neutral. "Tell us why," he says.

She looks at him the way Luke looks at me when I can't recite the latest Red Sox stats. She wonders if he's been living under a rock. "They robbed me of my church," she says. "*My* church. The church I was born and raised in. Now I'm without a place to worship. And I'm seventy-three. Too old to shop for a new one."

The judge looks like he might have a question, but Mrs. Rowlands doesn't wait for it. "I can't walk into a Catholic church without getting so angry I want to scream. Criminals, every last one of them."

The judge puts both hands up to stop her. "Mrs. Rowlands, surely you don't think *every* Catholic priest was involved in child molestation?"

"Involved? Oh, they were involved, all right. Those who weren't actively abusing protected the abusers, moved them from parish to parish, knowing a whole new crop of youngsters would be waiting at each one. While the children suffered, they protected their pals. Organized crime, plain and simple."

"But Mrs. Rowlands, many priests did neither. They didn't abuse children and they knew nothing about those who did."

"Oh, they knew," she says. "Don't kid yourself. It was there to be seen. They knew and they kept quiet. Cowards. Criminals and cowards." Her eyes dart around the room, daring any one of us to contradict her.

"Mrs. Rowlands," the judge takes a deep breath and exhales slowly, "let's talk about this particular case."

She shifts in her chair, adjusts her pocketbook.

"You understand, don't you, that this matter has nothing to do with the child-abuse scandal we've heard so much about lately?"

She nods.

"And you understand there's no child involved here?"

"I do," she says. "I realize that."

"So even though you're angry with the Catholic Church—as many people are—do you think you'd be able to put your anger aside if you were chosen to sit on this panel? Would you be able to base your decision solely on the evidence presented in the courtroom?"

She frowns, doesn't answer. Like Mr. Harmon, she seems to be giving it real thought. "I suppose so," she says at last.

Geraldine looks at each of us, then rolls her green eyes to the ceiling. *Fat chance,* she telegraphs.

"Thank you, Mrs. Rowlands," the judge says. "You may return to your seat in the jury box now."

She stands to leave and Clarence opens the chambers door for her. Geraldine begins her argument before it's shut. "Meyers and Rowlands," she says. "For cause."

"Harmon," Harry counters. "For cause."

"Meyers is out," the judge answers. "The other two stay."

"But, Judge," Harry argues, "Harmon thinks the dead guy walked on water. He's not going to be able to put that aside. I don't care what he says."

The judge shakes his head. "He said he would and I believe him. He went to one Mass two years ago. It's not enough."

"But Rowlands," Geraldine says. "She's already made up her mind about every Catholic priest. She told us so."

"She also told us she'd decide this case on the evidence presented, nothing else." Judge Gould stands and gathers his papers. We're done in here, it seems.

Harry and Geraldine both start in again, but the judge heads for the door. "If you feel that strongly," he says to both of them, "use a peremptory."

Nobody's happy. Geraldine storms out behind Judge Gould, Clarence in her wake. Harry gives my shoulder a little squeeze as he passes, his expression grim. Each side will be allowed just three peremptories at the conclusion of voir dire, three opportunities to oust a juror for no stated reason. No lawyer wants to waste a peremptory on a candidate who should be bounced for cause.

The judge is already on the bench by the time Harry and I reach our table. "Mrs. Meyers," he says, donning his glasses, "you are excused. Please report to the clerk's office for further instructions."

She stands and leaves the jury box, heads for the center aisle.

"And Mrs. Meyers . . ."

She stops and turns, looks up at Judge Gould. "Thank you," he says. She nods and continues her retreat.

"Mr. Harmon and Mrs. Rowlands," the judge says, "you may return to your seats in the gallery."

They both look somewhat surprised as they leave the box and head for the benches. I don't blame them. Impartiality is a slippery concept. And jury selection is a far cry from an exact science.

Dottie Bearse stands behind her desk, holding what looks like a small fishbowl. She draws consecutive slips of paper from it, reading a name from each, and one by one, fourteen potential jurors file into the box. Harry takes three blank sheets of legal-size paper from his file and hands two of them to me. Holliston looks hostile when I pass one to him with a pen. "It gets hard to keep them all straight after a while," I explain to him. "You might want to jot down their names and seat numbers."

His stare suggests I just asked him to draft a doctoral thesis in quantum physics. I turn away from him and face Dottie, who's delivering copies of the selected jurors' questionnaires to both tables. I divide my sheet into fourteen squares, each with a seat number, and fill in their names, ages, and occupations as the judge asks them all the boilerplate questions. *Does anyone work for law enforcement or have a relative or close friend who does? Has anyone been the victim of a violent crime? Does anyone know someone who has been?*

A couple of jurors are excused on the basis of their answers and Dottie pulls two more slips from her fishbowl. Robert Eastman and Alex Doane, both in their midfifties and wearing suits, fill the vacant seats. An investment banker and a nursing home administrator, both are dressed for work, hoping their time spent here today will be short, no doubt. Yes, they heard the questions asked of the others. No, neither of them has anything significant to report.

Judge Gould moves on to the legal standards jurors are expected to honor—the presumption of innocence, the burden of proof, the unanimous verdict. He asks if any of them will have difficulty accepting those parameters. Not a single hand goes up this time. Every last one of them plans to play by the rules. At this stage in the proceedings, most jurors believe they will.

The judge keeps Geraldine and Harry on a short leash as they ask their follow-up questions. In the end, neither of them has a valid challenge for cause as far as I can see, but Geraldine gets to her feet and announces she does. She always says she does. She can't help herself. "Number eight, Your Honor, for cause."

Juror number eight is a twenty-seven-year-old lobsterman from Hyannis. He told us in response to Geraldine's questions that his view of the Catholic Church in general is grim, the result of too many years spent in repressive parochial schools. He also said that view wouldn't affect his judgment in this case one whit. Geraldine doesn't have a leg to stand on here. Even she knows that, I think.

Judge Gould apparently thinks likewise. He smiles at her. "Not going to happen, Ms. Schilling."

She shakes her blond head at the injustice of it all and then exercises her first peremptory. The lobsterman takes his leave and his replacement answers all the preliminary questions. It's our turn now. "Mr. Madigan?" the judge says.

Harry leans forward on the table and arches his eyebrows at Holliston. It's routine to solicit opinions from criminal defendants during voir dire. And this particular defendant certainly seems to have some. He takes the pen I gave him earlier, reaches over to my diagram of the jury box, and draws a big X through the Margaret Murphy square. She's a fourth-grade teacher, an ex-nun.

"Are you sure?" Harry asks. "She's had some difficulties of her own with the Catholic Church, remember."

Holliston reaches in front of me again and draws another X on top of the first one. He's sure.

Harry excuses Margaret Murphy and she looks a little bit hurt as she leaves the box. Dottie pulls another slip from the fishbowl and we repeat the litany with Ms. Murphy's replacement. Geraldine exercises her second peremptory, dismissing a middle-aged woman from Wellfleet who confessed to a lifelong belief that Catholicism, with all its martyrs and miracles, is nothing more than myth. A tall, slender black man replaces her, a native of Haiti, according to his questionnaire.

Holliston stiffens at once. He grabs my diagram and draws an X through the newest candidate's box even before he sits down.

"Maybe we should let him answer a question first," I suggest.

Our client's stony expression tells me he can't imagine why I would propose such a thing. He pushes my diagram, with its new X, across the table toward Harry. Harry sighs and closes his eyes, but says nothing. He's not obligated to follow Holliston's instructions, of course. But as a practical matter, most criminal defense lawyers honor their clients' wishes when it comes to jury selection. We're choosing the decision-makers, after all. And it's the client who will live with the decision they reach.

Judge Gould walks through the preliminaries with the tall Haitian and then Harry dismisses him. Just like that. Without a single follow-up question. The dismissed juror doesn't react at all, but the judge does. He sees what's going on here and he's appalled, but there's not a damned thing he can do about it.

The ball is back in Geraldine's court. She stands but doesn't say anything, looking down at her table and tapping the eraser end of a pencil against her own hand-drawn diagram of the jury box. The third peremptory is always a difficult call. Pass on it and you give up an opportunity to improve your panel, to get rid of one more candidate who doesn't feel quite right. Exercise it and you may get stuck with a far worse juror from the gallery.

"Number two," she says at last. "The Commonwealth respectfully excuses juror number two."

I'm surprised. Juror number two is a sixty-year-old carpenter from Dennis who told us he views the Catholic Church's insistence that its priests remain celibate as "abnormal." Otherwise, though, he has no feelings about the church one way or the other. If I were in Geraldine's shoes—and I was for many years—I'd keep him. I wouldn't run the risk of ending up with someone more opinionated in his place.

The carpenter exits and Dottie pulls yet another slip from the dwindling supply in her glass bowl. "Cora Rowlands," she announces. Geraldine actually groans.

Harry and I twist in our seats to watch the newest candidate approach from the back row. Geraldine turns completely around, her back to the judge, to do the same. No doubt she's hoping to see a female Rowlands *other* than the woman we heard from in chambers. Too bad for Geraldine.

Cora nods to each of us as she walks between our tables and then crosses the front of the room to the box, settling in the second seat, front row. The jury box seats are narrower than the chairs in chambers; her pocketbook doesn't fit between the armrests. She sets it on the floor at her feet and purses her lips, unhappy with the accommodations.

"Your Honor," Geraldine intones, "the Commonwealth renews its motion to dismiss this juror for cause, based on the content of her comments in chambers."

Geraldine doesn't have a prayer. I can't blame her for trying, though, for attempting to undo the damage she did when she used that last peremptory. We've all been there, most of us more than once.

Judge Gould shakes his head. "I've already ruled on that, Counsel. And the ruling stands."

Cora Rowlands looks from the judge to Geraldine, hands clasped on her lap, shoulders erect. Her expression says: *So there.*

Geraldine pretends she doesn't notice. I know her, though; she does. She remains on her feet, looking like she has more to say on the matter, even when Judge Gould moves on. He runs quickly through the preliminaries with Cora and then turns his attention to Harry. "Mr. Madigan, anything further?"

Holliston takes his pen and reaches over to my diagram again. He draws an X through the number-one box and another through number seven—opposite ends of the front row—Anthony Laurino and Maria Marzetti. Maria is the woman Holliston identified as a *cat-lick* as soon as he arrived this morning.

"We don't get two more," I tell him. "We get one. Three total."

He looks at me and his eyebrows fuse. He's certain I'm lying, it seems, cheating him out of a fair shake.

"Pick one," I say. "Believe it or not, the Rules of Criminal Procedure aren't going to change in the next five minutes, not even for you."

"Hold on," Harry tells both of us. "This is a mistake. We've got a decent panel right now. Why take a chance on making it worse?"

He's right, of course, but Holliston doesn't think so. He takes his pen and darkens the X over juror number one. Anthony Laurino must go. It seems an Italian male is even more objectionable than an Italian female. I've no idea what rationale is at work here. But I do know our exercise of peremptories bears a frightening resemblance to ethnic cleansing.

Even so, Harry seems prepared to let our client call the shots.

These men and women will determine Derrick Holliston's fate, after all. Harry shakes his head and leans close to me. "Are we forgetting anyone?" he whispers. "I'd hate like hell to leave a left-handed Latvian in the room." He stands and perfunctorily bounces Anthony Laurino.

After meeting the judge's less-than-happy stare, Harry drops back into his chair, kneading his temples. The newest dismissed juror doesn't mind a bit, though. He looks relieved, happy even, as he leaves the courtroom. Dottie draws another slip from the few left in her bowl and announces: "Gregory Harmon." Harry plants his elbows on the table, buries his face in both hands.

Holliston stares at our final juror, in flannel shirt and work boots, as he walks to the front of the room. When Mr. Harmon settles into the number-one spot in the box, right next to Cora Rowlands, our client clicks his pen and sets it on the table. "There," he says to no one in particular. "That's better."

Chapter 9

For attorneys in the midst of trials—particularly defense attorneys in the midst of criminal trials—lunch breaks have little to do with food. Unless, of course, the attorney is Harry Madigan. We're at the Piccadilly Deli, waiting for his mega–meatball sub with extra mozzarella and a gallon of Tabasco. We take seats at our usual spot—near the front windows—and slide today's *Cape Cod Times* to one side of the table's mottled red Formica surface. Harry downs a quart of chocolate milk. I sip my coffee and call the office.

The Kydd answers on the third ring. "Marty," he says as soon as he hears my voice, "this is nuts. We need a secretary."

He's right; we do. The three of us have been operating without administrative help for two years now. It's getting old.

"Well, why didn't you say so sooner, Kydd? I'll hire one today. Della Street, if she hasn't retired yet."

Harry opened our South Chatham office a couple of years ago, after spending two decades as a public defender. I joined him within weeks, having resigned from a ten-year stint with the District Attorney's office six months earlier. We recruited Kevin Kydd—then in his second year of practice—right out from under Geraldine's nose. She's still sore about it—and with good reason. The Kydd's a keeper.

"I'm not joking," he says. "I've spent the entire day talking to walk-ins and fielding phone calls. I'm getting zero done here."

I know how frustrated he is; I've been there. But between the substandard hourly rates paid on court appointments and the fee forfeitures we face in drug cases, the office isn't exactly a cash cow these days. "Hang in there," I tell him. "We're hoping to bring an administrative person on board in the new year—part-time, at least."

A deli worker delivers Harry's sub to our table—a perk reserved for the regulars—and Harry grabs a second quart of chocolate milk from the cooler. He also takes a cranberry muffin from the basket on top and puts it in front of me, even though he knows better. I don't eat lunch during trials; my stomach doesn't allow it. He takes an enormous bite of his foot-long feast and then leans over to read while I jot down a list of the phone calls we've missed so far today: eight for him; a half dozen for me.

"And the Senator," the Kydd says. "He called just before you did."

"Kendrick?" The question isn't necessary, of course. There aren't many senators on my Rolodex.

"How did you know?" The Kydd oozes sincerity. I don't get away with much in our circle.

"Lucky guess," I tell him. "What did the good Senator want?"

"He needs to see you. He's coming in this afternoon."

"I won't get back until after five. Probably closer to six."

"I told him that," the Kydd answers, "but he insisted. Says it's important that he see you today."

"Did he say why?"

"Nope. Once he found out when you'd be back here, he seemed anxious to get off the phone."

It occurs to me that the Commonwealth's senior senator is frequently anxious to get off the phone.

"Wish they all felt that way," the Kydd adds. "Every other joker who calls this joint wants to tell me his life's story."

"Have you had lunch?"

Like Harry, the Kydd tends to get pretty cranky when he misses a meal. "Lunch?" he bellows. "I haven't had time to pour a second cup of coffee. How the hell would I have gotten lunch?"

"Order in," I tell him. "And put it on the tab."

Harry and I have an open account with Cape Wok, Chatham's only Chinese takeout. The food's pretty good and they deliver. It's one of our heftier monthly expenses.

"Oh, I get it," the Kydd says. "Szechwan duck will fix everything. Throw in a little pork fried rice and I won't *mind* spending my days in the secretarial pool."

"Eat," I tell him. "We'll see you in a few hours."

He's still complaining when I snap my cell phone shut.

Harry swallows the last of his sandwich, drains the milk carton, and then dumps his trash in the bin. I stand to put on my coat, but his stricken expression stops me.

"What?" I ask.

"We can't leave yet," he says.

"We can't?"

"No way." He carries his empty tray to the counter, exchanges a few words with the clerk, and then hurries back to our table.

"Is there a reason?" I ask.

He unwraps my cranberry muffin, pops a third of it into his mouth, and then leans down to whisper, as if he doesn't want the other customers to hear. "They have apple pie," he says at last. "And it's warm."

CHAPTER 10

"An ice pick," Geraldine says. She's seated at her table, next to Clarence, motionless. She was in that spot when the rest of us left for the break at two and she was there when we got back an hour later. This isn't normal. Geraldine Schilling rarely sits; her metabolism doesn't allow it. Everyone involved in this case seems unusually troubled by it. Everyone except Derrick Holliston, that is.

The courtroom isn't filled to capacity, but it's close. More than a hundred people sit in the gallery's benches—plus the twenty of us up here in front. Even so, there's not a sound in the room as we all wait for her to continue. She swivels her chair toward the jurors now and steeples her hands beneath her chin. "Our Medical Examiner will tell you that Father Francis Patrick McMahon was stabbed to death with an ice pick."

The pause is so long that a person who doesn't know our District Attorney might think she has nothing more to say. That person would be wrong; Geraldine *always* has more to say. She wheels her chair back, away from the table, and stands. "Stabbed," she repeats. "Eight times."

Fourteen pairs of eyes remain fixed on her as she takes slow, deliberate steps toward the jury box. No one blinks.

"Three times in the left shoulder." She holds up one finger, then a second, then a third. "Twice in the right." She adds her little finger, then her thumb, and falls silent again, her raised right hand rigid as if she's about to take an oath.

Maria Marzetti closes her eyes. Cora Rowlands does too, then bites her lower lip. No one else moves.

"Twice in the upper abdomen," Geraldine says at last. She uses both hands now to continue the count. "And once . . ."

She abandons her finger tally and leans on the rail of the jury box.

". . . directly into the aorta."

Most of them react. A few shake their heads; others cover their mouths. All but two look away from Geraldine—at their laps, at the ceiling, at the floor—as they absorb the information she's giving them. Side-by-side stoic souls in the back row, though—Robert Eastman and Alex Doane—remain immobile, arms folded across their suit coats.

"Dr. Ramsey will tell you that Father Francis Patrick McMahon bled to death in minutes. He was dead less than an hour when his body was discovered by his pastor."

Calvin Ramsey has been Barnstable County's Medical Examiner for a year and a half. He's a meticulous scientist, a persuasive witness. His report nails Holliston—to the corpse, to the scene, and to the weapon—six ways from Sunday. The doctor won't comment on the self-defense claim, of course. He can't.

"Dr. Ramsey will also tell you that blood samples taken from the crime scene came from two sources."

Geraldine turns her back to the jurors now, and walks slowly across the room to our table. It's time to point. In every murder trial, there comes a time for the prosecutor to point. And no prosecutor does it more effectively than Geraldine Schilling.

"Most of it came from the deceased," she says. "But some, trace amounts, came from this man."

Holliston looks directly at her index finger as if he's staring down the barrel of a shotgun. And he is.

"He admits it," she says, turning back to face the panel, her finger still inches from Holliston's face. "He admits stabbing the priest to death. But he wants you to say it's okay."

Harry shifts in his seat, one hand on the edge of our table, the other clutching his armrest. She's inching toward improper territory; he's preparing to pounce.

"This man," she says, still pointing, "wants you to say Father Francis Patrick McMahon deserved it."

Harry explodes as he jumps to his feet. The gavel pounds the desk three times before he finishes the word *objection*. Judge Gould is a step ahead of him.

The judge is on his feet too. "Attorney Schilling, you know better." He's not shouting, exactly, but he's close. He and Geraldine have a history.

"Move for an instruction, Your Honor." Harry's shaking his head at the inadequacy of the remedy even as he asks for it. He'll get the instruction. But the damage is done. The words can't be unspoken.

"The jury will disregard the prosecutor's last comment," Judge Gould tells the panel, "in its entirety."

They nod at him, most wearing earnest expressions. They'll disregard the comment. Or at least they think they will.

The judge sits again, his attention back to Geraldine. "One more remark like that, Counsel, and your opening statement is over."

"My apologies to the Court, Your Honor."

Baloney. Her apologies are offered strictly to mollify the jury. Every lawyer in the room knows that, including Judge Gould. "Move on," he says, frowning at her.

Harry sits as Geraldine walks back toward the panel.

"After Dr. Ramsey testifies," she says, "you'll hear from Chatham's Chief of Police, Thomas Fitzpatrick. He'll tell you it took a full week to assemble the forensic evidence necessary to file the appropriate charges. Chief Fitzpatrick will tell you this defendant told his tall tale immediately—as soon as the police stormed his apartment. The Chief will also tell you this defendant told no one about the alleged sexual assault until that time. He sought no medical care. He sought no assistance of any kind. An entire week had passed. And he told no one about the trauma he claims to have suffered. Think about that."

She pauses so they can.

Harry grips the edge of our table, poised to pounce once more. Her job is to give them a road map of the evidence she intends to present, not to argue about what it does or doesn't mean. Not now, anyway.

"Think about the fact that this defendant"—she points at Holliston yet again, from across the room, and raises her voice for the first time today—"claims he was sexually assaulted by Father McMahon, claims a physical altercation ensued, an altercation so

76

serious he had no choice but to stab the older man in self-defense. Eight times, remember."

Every juror nods. They remember.

"And then he told no one. For a week." She plants herself in front of the box and turns to stare at Holliston. He gazes straight ahead, the blank look on his face suggesting he's unaware she's talking about him. "He told no one until he was charged with murder. He told no one until he needed an excuse."

Harry gets to his feet.

Judge Gould holds up both hands, palms out; an objection isn't necessary. Once again, Geraldine is at the outer boundary of proper opening. The judge doesn't plan to wait until she steps over it this time. "Counsel," he says. He removes his glasses and massages the bridge of his nose. "Move on."

She looks up at him and smiles, as if that's precisely what she had in mind, but she doesn't answer. She turns to the panel instead. "And finally," she says, "you'll hear from Monsignor Dominic Davis, the pastor of St. Veronica's Parish."

Harry drops back into his chair.

Geraldine leans on the rail of the jury box and turns to stare at Holliston yet again. "Monsignor Davis will tell you in no uncertain terms that the defendant's claims are false. He'll tell you they're ridiculous. He'll tell you Father McMahon never assaulted anyone, sexually or otherwise, in his fifty-seven years of life. The pastor will tell you the deceased was a man of God, a man of principle, a man of peace."

She turns and walks toward us. "Now I can't tell you," she says, "whether or not you will hear from this defendant. He's under no obligation to testify." She stops in front of our table, studies Holliston as if he's a still life, then does a U-turn and walks toward the jurors again. "But I can tell you this: you will hear his story; you will hear his version of the events that transpired in St. Veronica's sacristy last Christmas Eve. You will hear it even if he doesn't take the witness stand—because it's what he told the police officers when he was arrested. His story is part of their report."

Geraldine Schilling is good at what she does.

"And the rules of evidence dictate that if part of a police report is admitted into evidence, the rest of that report comes in as well—even if part of it was manufactured by the accused. Bear in mind, as you listen to the recitation of events as described by the defendant, that it's nothing more than that. His recitation. His story. His belated attempt to justify a senseless, vicious murder."

With that, she nods up at the judge, fires a final glare in Holliston's direction, and reclaims her seat next to Clarence.

Judge Gould checks the pendulum clock hanging on the wall behind the jury box. "Ladies and gentlemen," he says, "we'll hear from the defense now. After that, we'll adjourn for the day. We'll begin with witnesses in the morning."

Harry stands, buttons his suit coat, and takes a halfhearted stab at straightening his tie. Holliston gets to his feet as well. I reach up and take hold of his jacket sleeve, to tell him to stay put. This isn't the seventh-inning stretch, after all.

Holliston shakes my hand away and steps out from behind the table. Harry looks over at him, then down at me, and I shrug. I don't know what the hell our client's up to. And then—in a millisecond—I do.

"Siddown, Madigan," he says as he struts toward the jury box. "You're fired."

CHAPTER 11

Geraldine paces around Judge Gould's chambers like a woman possessed. She stops short, faces the judge, and plants her hands on her narrow hips. "He can't do this," she says, exhaling so hard her blond bangs billow.

She knows better. He can. Like every criminal defendant who's compos mentis, Derrick Holliston is entitled to represent himself if he so chooses, even if it amounts to tactical suicide. It's a constitutional guarantee. It's a judicial headache. And it's a prosecutorial nightmare.

The newly *pro se* defendant helped himself to a seat as soon as we filed in here. Two guards keep watch on either side of him, standing just inches from his chair, hands clasped behind their backs, gazes focused on their prisoner. Clarence, Harry, and I are lined up against the side wall. Even Judge Gould is on his feet, leaning against the bookcase behind his desk. "Mr. Holliston," he says, his tone grave, "I urge you to reconsider."

Holliston snorts. The judge's advice seems to rate right up there with Harry's. "That's what I did," he says. "I reconsidered. I don't want no lawyer. I want the job done right. So I'm gonna do it myself."

"The ramifications of this decision will follow you for the rest of your life," the judge tells him. "Taking this step will dramatically increase the likelihood of conviction. And if you are convicted of first-degree murder, you'll spend the rest of your earthly days behind bars. I'm sure your lawyers have explained that to you."

Holliston wags a finger at Judge Gould. "*Used-to-be* lawyers," he says. "My used-to-be lawyers explained that to me. And I don't like the idea of spending the rest of my *earthly days* behind bars." He imitates the judge's inflection when he repeats his words. "I don't like it one bit. That's why I'm my lawyer now."

The judge sighs and turns to Harry.

Harry shrugs and looks up at the ceiling. "He's a big boy. He's made his decision. Let him live with it."

Not exactly what the judge was hoping to hear.

"Mr. Holliston," I try, "if there are specific issues you're worried about, particular facts you want brought out during trial, I'm sure Mr. Madigan will accommodate you. You can have all the input you want without giving up the benefit of counsel."

He snorts again, louder this time. My advice ranks a rung or two below the judge's, it seems. "*Benefit?*" he says, pointing at Harry. "Ex-cu-uze me, but I don't see no *benefit* with this counsel."

"Mr. Holliston, you don't have a clue." Geraldine pivots in her spiked heels to face him. "You don't have any idea what you're in for if you go forward *pro se*."

He juts his chin upward and sneers, inviting her to fill him in.

She pauses and glances at the court reporter, who's perched on his stool beside the judge's desk, tapping away. No doubt she's weighing what she wants to say in the heat of the moment against the eventual impact her words will have on appeal.

"I'll bury you," she says.

To hell with the appeal.

"Don't think we're going to handle you with kid gloves," she continues. "You'll be held to the same standards every *real* lawyer is held to in that courtroom." She points to the chambers door. "And I'll shut you down every time you fall short."

Holliston yawns. He's unimpressed.

"And you will fall short," she tells him, her green eyes ablaze. "At every turn. I guarantee it."

Judge Gould pulls his chair out from the desk and sits. "Look," he says to Holliston, "we can't stop you. If you're determined to represent yourself, you have an absolute right to do it. No one in this room can stop you."

Our ex-client almost smiles. At last, an acknowledgment of his vast power. He pounds his palms on the armrests and slides to the edge of his chair. "That's right," he says, looking pleased that the judge finally figured it out. "So let's get on with it."

Judge Gould shakes his head. "Not so fast. We can't stop you from taking your defense into your own hands. But we can stop you from doing it today."

Holliston looks confused, then annoyed, his brief moment of omnipotence abruptly ended.

The judge checks his watch. "It's late," he says. "I'm going to dismiss the jurors for the day. If you're still sure of your decision in the morning, sir, you may deliver your opening statement then."

Holliston looks like he wants to argue, but Judge Gould doesn't give him a chance. "Mr. Madigan, Ms. Nickerson," he says as he stands, "I want you in the courtroom throughout trial."

Holliston stands too, and his escorts inch closer to him. His expression is satisfied now. Overall, he's pleased with the results of our powwow.

The judge continues talking to Harry and me as he heads for the door. "I want you waiting in the wings," he says, "ready to advise when necessary, ready to jump back on board if the defendant changes his mind."

He reaches for the doorknob, then stops. "And Mr. Holliston," he says, turning to face him.

Holliston stares back at him, signature sneer in place.

"I sincerely hope you will."

CHAPTER 12

Harry and I pull into our newly plowed office driveway at five, earlier than either of us expected to be back. Charles Kendrick is already here, though. The Senator's enormous gray Humvee is parked next to my tired Thunderbird. Harry cuts the Jeep's engine and jumps out, eager to play GI Joe with our senior senator's tank.

He strolls around in the falling snow—seemingly oblivious to the biting wind—peering through the Hummer's windows and whistling. "Damn," he says, running his gloved hand along the hood. "I could *live* in this thing."

"No, you couldn't," I correct him as I head for the old farmhouse. "You don't have enough furniture. And the rent would kill you."

The Kydd is seated behind the antique pine table in the front office, just hanging up the telephone, two almost empty Cape Wok cartons in front of him. He points to the ceiling with his coffee mug as soon as I close the door and then scrawls on a yellow legal pad: *nervous breakdown in progress.* Senator Kendrick is upstairs in my office, and apparently he's not doing well. I hang my damp parka on the coatrack and head for the wrought-iron spiral staircase. Harry hasn't come inside yet. He's still hovering around the Hummer, I suppose, mentally moving in.

Senator Kendrick is standing, gazing out the double-hung rear windows, taking in the view behind our farmhouse-turned-office-building: an open field, a small stand of scrub pines, and the salty water of Taylor's Pond in the distance. He wheels around when I reach the top step and shoves both hands deep into his pants pockets, seemingly embarrassed to have been caught alone with his own thoughts. "Marty," he says, his tone suggesting he's been waiting all day, "you're here."

Can't argue with that. I gesture toward the slip-covered couch against the far wall and he takes a seat on one end of it. I slide my briefcase onto a corner of the cluttered desk, drape my suit jacket over the leather chair, and then join him. He leans forward when I sit, elbows on his knees, head lowered, fists clenched. The Kydd's assessment was accurate. This is a man in crisis.

"What's wrong?" I ask. "What's happened?"

"Nothing," he answers too quickly, then stares down at the worn, braided rug.

I don't believe him. But I don't say so.

"There are things I haven't told you," he continues. "And I should."

He pauses, seems to grope for words. I wait.

"Things you should know," he adds at last.

"And you just realized this today?" I'm pretty sure I know what he's decided to tell me, of course, but I don't let on. He should do the talking.

"Yes," he says. "I'm sorry. I should have leveled with you at the outset."

He pauses again. And again I wait.

"About Michelle Forrester." He looks pained when he says her name. His eyes meet mine for the first time today, then dart to my empty desk chair. "Look, there's no delicate way to put this."

"Don't worry about delicate," I tell him. "Just give me the facts."

"We had an affair," he says quietly, reexamining the rug.

I nod and wait for him to continue.

"It went on for about a year. And then my wife found out."

"How?"

He shakes his head and sighs. "She and Abby went to San Francisco to spend a week with my in-laws. Michelle stayed with me in Boston for part of that time."

"In Boston?" When they're not in Washington, D.C., or Chatham, the Kendricks live on a frequently photographed hillside estate in Concord. I didn't know they had a place in Boston as well.

"I keep an apartment there," he says. "I have for years. I'm in the city a lot for political events and fund-raisers. Sometimes I'm just too damned tired to drive home afterward."

That makes sense. But taking Michelle Forrester there sure as hell didn't. I raise my eyebrows at him.

"I know," he says. "It was stupid. But remember, we couldn't go to a hotel. Or even a restaurant."

He's right, of course. They would have been on the front page of every rag in the nation if they had.

"In any event," he says, "Honey had a tiff with her mother, cut the visit short by a couple of days. She and Abby flew into Logan late one night and decided to stay at the apartment, drive out to Concord in the morning." He looks up at me and shakes his head, then closes his eyes. "It was ugly," he mutters.

"How long ago?"

He leans back against the couch, stretches his long legs, and faces me. "Four months. Just before Abby went back to school."

And just as rumors of his potential bid for the Democratic nomination were reaching a crescendo. I keep that thought to myself. "What happened?" I ask.

He half laughs. "What didn't happen? Tears. Threats. Tantrums. And not just Honey. Abby too. I swear, sometimes those two seem more like sisters than mother and daughter. There's not a dinner plate left in the place."

"But your wife didn't leave you."

"No," he says. "I begged her not to. I swore I'd end it with Michelle. And I did. That day."

"Okay." I stand and cross the room, my back to him, then take the chair behind my desk. "You don't need me to tell you this is going to come out, Senator. Law enforcement will analyze every detail of Michelle Forrester's existence with a fine-tooth comb before this is over. Sooner or later, they'll get to you."

"Sooner," he says.

"Pardon?"

It's his turn to stand now. He walks toward the two upholstered wing chairs facing my desk, leans on the back of one, and stares down at his clasped hands. "Sooner," he repeats. "They'll get to me sooner, not later."

"There's more."

He nods. "We were together Thursday night," he says, "the night before she disappeared."

Sometimes I think no client can say anything to surprise me anymore. Other times, I know better.

"It wasn't planned," he continues, not looking at me. "She stopped by the Old Harbor Road house after she finished at Four Cs."

"Four Cs" is local parlance for Cape Cod Community College—the last place Michelle Forrester was seen by anyone who's come forward. Anyone other than the Senator, I realize now.

"Hold it." I raise my hands to stop him. "She was in Hyannis. She was due in Stamford, Connecticut, the next morning. Are you telling me she drove a half hour in the wrong direction for an impromptu visit?"

He nods again, a faint smile on his face. "That's exactly what I'm telling you. She knew Honey and Abby weren't coming to the Cape until the next day, knew I'd be at the house alone. She showed up at about seven. She was quite pleased with the way the press conference had gone. I was too; I'd just watched parts of it on the news. Michelle wanted to talk about it. I fixed her a drink."

He shrugs, as if the rest was inevitable.

"What time did she leave?"

"Before six," he says, "the next morning."

"In the dark."

"That's right." He meets my gaze now. "We have a neighbor—in the bungalow behind our place. She's a year-rounder."

Let's hope she's a blind year-rounder.

"Michelle and I had spent time at the Chatham house before," he says. "She always parked in the garage, left before daybreak, kept her headlights off until she reached the main road."

"Give me a minute," I tell him. I plant my elbows on the desk and knead my temples. I wish I had eaten the damned cranberry muffin at the Piccadilly Deli a few hours ago. My head aches.

Senator Kendrick straightens, walks around the chair he's been leaning on, and drops into it. "I'm sorry," he repeats. "I know I should have told you sooner. But I kept thinking we'd hear from Michelle."

His eyes meet mine when I look up and the emotion in them is genuine. He's beyond worried; he's terrified. "I just didn't think anything bad had happened to her," he says. "But now I'm afraid I was wrong."

CHAPTER 13

The neighbor isn't blind, as it turns out. She's deaf. Helene Wilson greeted me at her kitchen door with a broad smile, a notepad and a pen. When I started to explain my uninvited appearance on her doorstep, she shook her head at me. "I'm deaf," she said, handing the pen and paper to me. "You'll have to use this."

I wrote my name, then a short message explaining my role as her neighbor's attorney. She invited me inside at once, and the clarity of her speech took me by surprise. It gave no hint that her world is silent.

"My deafness," she says now, as if reading my mind, "is relatively new. Until a few years ago, my hearing was perfect."

What happened? I write on the notepad.

She takes my parka and scarf, hangs them on a hook to the side of the door, and shrugs. "I'm what's known as a late deafened adult," she says. "There are more of us around than most people realize."

This is news to me. Again, she seems to read my mind.

"There are so many of us, in fact, that the Association of Late Deafened Adults has fifteen chapters throughout the United States. Our most famous member is King Jordan, the president of Gallaudet University. But all the members are like me: folks born into the hearing world, enjoying the pleasures sound brings to life—music, laughter, rainfall—and then it all starts to fade. The process gains momentum until—poof!—one day sound is gone. Completely."

Look out, King Jordan. Having known her all of three minutes, I'm willing to bet Helene Wilson will be the association's most famous member before long. She delivers her history without a shred of self-pity, with an "ain't that the darnedest thing you ever heard" expression on her face. A fifty-something, blue-eyed blonde who's probably five feet on her tiptoes, she's got *hot ticket* written all over her. She leads the way through a galley kitchen and into a softly lit living room, then directs me to the sofa with a sweep of her hand.

Her place is compact—smaller than my Windmill Lane cottage, even—but it's huge on charm. I've noticed this bungalow from the outside many times, even before I got the first worried phone calls from the Senator next door. It has access to all the same outdoor amenities of the Kendrick estate—the drop-dead views, the stilt-legged shorebirds, the salt-laden winds—all with a fraction of the upkeep. My kind of real estate.

The living room is richly decorated in a colorful Southwestern motif, warmed by a crackling fire. A pair of glasses sits on top of an open hardback on the coffee table, a half-filled goblet of red wine next to it. "Can I get you anything?" Helene gestures toward a wet bar at the other end of the room. "A cocktail, maybe?"

I shake my head. It's late; I want to get home, put on a pair of old sweats, have a snack and a glass of wine on my own living room couch. *I won't stay long,* I write on the notepad. *Thanks for seeing me.*

The sofa is upholstered in a soft, taupe corduroy. Helene joins me on it, her eyes openly curious. "What can I do for you?" she says.

I hesitate for a moment. For some reason, having to pen my words makes me want to choose them more carefully. *I'm looking into the disappearance of Michelle Forrester,* I write at last.

Her bright expression darkens as she reads. "A terrible thing," she says, shaking her head. "Her people must be worried sick."

I nod.

"If I can help," she adds, "I certainly will."

Time to face the music. I'll never get the answer if I don't ask the question. And it's why I came here, after all. *When was the last time you saw her?* I scrawl.

Helene Wilson's hesitation speaks volumes. She knows at least as much as any of us, perhaps more. "You're his lawyer," she says finally, "so whatever I tell you stays between you, me, and the Senator, is that right?"

Technically, it's not; the privilege exists only between attorney and client. It doesn't extend to communications with third parties. I shake my head and Helene looks surprised. *I can't guarantee that,* I write. *But remember, I'm Senator Kendrick's lawyer. Nothing you say that's adverse to his interests will go anywhere else. Not if I can help it.*

She hesitates again, considering my written message, and I'm touched by the depth of her loyalty to her neighbor. "Michelle was here last Thursday night," she says at last. She points out her side window, toward Senator Kendrick's estate. "Next door."

There it is. And it's only a matter of time before some Chatham detective is sitting where I am. Two, probably. *Did you see her arrive?* I write.

"Not exactly," she says.

I arch my eyebrows.

"She got here around seven," Helene continues. "I remember because I'd just finished watching the news and Michelle had been on it. She and the Senator had held a press conference at Four Cs that day." Helene points toward a distressed-pine corner cupboard that houses a modest TV. "Closed captioning," she adds, smiling. "It's not perfect, but it usually gets the job done."

She's two steps ahead of me. *Not exactly,* I write. *You didn't exactly see her arrive. What do you mean?*

She shrugs. "It was dark," she says, "so I didn't see Michelle pull in. But her car passed in front of my house." She points over her shoulder, out the window behind us.

I'm still for a moment, and Helene seems to sense my questions, one of them anyhow. "Michelle's car has been here before," she says, "many times. She always keeps her headlights off when she travels this lane, but I know when she comes and goes. She drives a sporty, foreign number. I know the feel of it."

I'm not sure how to ask her what that means. My pen is still.

"Not for a while, though," Helene adds. "Until last Thursday, it had been months since Michelle Forrester had been here. Not since the end of the summer."

Helene Wilson knows what she's talking about; her time line

dovetails with the Senator's. I still don't get it, though. *How? I write on a new page. How did you know a car was driving by in the dark? And how did you know it was Michelle's?*

Her grin tells me she's been asked questions like this one before—more than a few times—and she expects a healthy dose of skepticism from her listener. "I have five senses," she says. "Just not the same five you have."

None of my five is particularly keen right now.

"I know when an animal passes by in the dark," she continues. "And I usually know what kind of animal it is—long before I grab my flashlight to check. On occasion, I confuse a coyote with a dog, but I never misidentify a deer. Automobiles are much easier by comparison. It's all about vibration. Sound *is* vibration, after all."

I know that—and I believe what she's telling me—but I still don't understand. I hold up my hand so she'll pause. *Are you saying you can tell the particular type of car that's driving by?* I write. *Even if you don't see it?*

She laughs. "No," she says. "I'm not that good. But I do know when it's the Senator's. That Humvee of his is no ordinary car. Talk about vibration."

I stop her again. *But you said you knew Michelle's.*

"Only because I know her pattern," she says. "She keeps her headlights out, comes and goes in total darkness."

I'm quiet for a moment, digesting the fact that Michelle Forrester's cover is what gives her away—to this astute neighbor, anyhow.

"The Senator pulled in at around five-thirty that afternoon," Helene says. "Michelle arrived just after seven."

My pen is paralyzed again. It won't take much longer for the Chatham cops to unearth this information. Once they do, they'll take it straight to Geraldine. And though she already knows about the affair, I'm certain she has no idea Michelle was with the Senator the night before she disappeared. When that fact comes to light, Charles Kendrick will have some explaining to do.

"She left early the next morning," Helene adds. "And I saw her little hot rod that time. She left a bit later than she normally does. It was starting to get light already."

I'm still wordless, written or otherwise, but a wave of relief washes over me. My client faces an outraged wife and a political scandal. But this last piece of information from Helene Wilson should ultimately shield him from our District Attorney, at least. I pull a business card from my wallet and hand it to her. *If you think of anything else,* I write.

She puts a hand on my forearm to stop me. "I'll let you know," she finishes for me. "And I mean it," she says, tucking my card into her sweater pocket. "I will. I'm not the least bit afraid to get involved."

I don't doubt that for a minute. Something tells me Helene Wilson isn't afraid of much.

CHAPTER 14

Thursday, December 16

Big Red hustles out the side door as soon as Judge Gould's eyes give him the go-ahead. Derrick Holliston has made up his mind. He'll represent himself. He's every bit as determined this morning as he was in chambers yesterday.

"Mr. Holliston," the judge says as the door clicks shut behind the bailiff, "you're absolutely certain about this?"

At least Holliston has the good sense to stand as he replies. "Hell, yeah," he says. Geraldine groans.

My bet is that's the first of many groans we'll hear from Geraldine Schilling during the next couple of days. No prosecutor wants to take on a *pro se* defendant; it's a lose-lose proposition. If she hammers on Holliston for every mistake he makes, he'll rarely finish a thought; the jurors will likely think she's a bully. If she doesn't, he'll muddy the record—and the jurors' minds—with all sorts of information that doesn't belong there. To add to her conundrum, any objections Geraldine forgoes here will be waived for good. If she decides to let a few of Holliston's mistakes slide—to avoid looking like a bully—those issues are lost once and for all. The Court of Appeals won't consider an argument that isn't raised in the trial court first.

Harry and I pack up and move to the bar, where the half dozen chairs reserved for attorneys are empty. They're the only seats in the house that are. Every row in the gallery is packed, even the pair of deacon's benches in the small loft at the far end of the room. And, according to Big Red, a sizable spillover crowd is already assembled in one of the basement conference rooms, where the proceedings will be aired on closed-circuit TV.

Holliston stands, wheels the two chairs Harry and I had been using away from the defense table, and parks them against the side wall. He centers his own chair and then settles into it, neither a pen nor a shred of paper in front of him. He's sculpting a scene for the jurors, one with a message: The world is against him. And he's all alone.

"Crazy like a fox," Harry whispers.

Big Red returns, the jurors single file behind him. Most look surprised as they enter the courtroom, their eyes wide as they take in the sea of spectators. I twist in my chair to absorb the scene with them, and I spot dozens of familiar faces. The front benches are peppered with press. The whole room is sprinkled with Chatham residents, many of them undoubtedly St. Veronica's parishioners. And dead center in the front row, directly behind Harry and me, sits Bobby "the Butcher" Frazier.

The Butcher's straight black hair is slicked back, and the top half of his white dress shirt is unbuttoned, the collar spread wide. He wears no undershirt, despite the December cold. And there's a reason, I realize after a moment. A few inches of his scar are visible, below the right shoulder, bisected by a solitary gold chain. The scar is raised and uneven, lighter in color than the rest of his swarthy skin. My eyes move to his and he meets them with a steady gaze. The Butcher would like to be a part of this trial. He'd like to be Exhibit A.

Judge Gould bids the jurors good morning and they all return the greeting. Most look more relaxed today than they did yesterday, their surroundings not quite so foreign now. Robert Eastman and Alex Doane, the investment banker and nursing home administrator, have traded their suits for more casual attire. Eastman sports a front-zip gray sweatshirt, Doane a black turtleneck. Neither of them has any delusions about making it into work today.

Cora Rowlands seems more at ease too, her coatdress replaced by navy blue slacks and a cream-colored tunic. Her silver bouffant is freshly teased and the large satchel she carted around yesterday is nowhere in sight. Big Red probably found a secure cubby for it, putting Cora's concerns about the close contours of the jury box to rest.

Maria Marzetti looks downright sultry in a low-cut maroon sweater and black skirt, a fact not lost on the thirty-something general contractor in the back row. He stares at her profile while she and the others give their undivided attention to the judge. They're ready to get to work. Thirteen of them, anyway.

"Ladies and gentlemen," Judge Gould says, leaning forward on the bench, "there's been a change in plans."

Gregory Harmon is the only juror who seems to have noticed already. He's dressed as he was yesterday—jeans, flannel shirt, and work boots—and he looks comfortable in the number-one seat. He glances at our ex-client alone at the defense table, then back at Harry and me, and then at Cora Rowlands beside him. Harmon's expression is curious, nothing more.

"The defendant has chosen to represent himself," the judge continues, "and he's entitled to do so. You're to draw no inference from his decision, entertain no speculation about it."

All of them look at Holliston now, then at us. No doubt they're wondering why Harry and I are still in the courtroom. The judge won't tell them—he won't say anything to draw attention to the safety net he's provided—but they'll figure it out. And Geraldine will remind them of our presence every time Holliston gives her an opening. My gut tells me he'll give her more than a few.

"At this time, ladies and gentlemen," Judge Gould takes his glasses off and leans back in his tall, leather chair, "the defendant will deliver his opening statement."

Holliston stands and runs both hands down the front of his suit coat, then starts toward the jury box. I can't see his face from where we're sitting—he's walking away from us—but the jurors' expressions tell me he's making eye contact with them, one by one, as he crosses the room. He's given his performance some thought, it seems. He stops a couple of feet from the box, squares his shoulders and clasps his hands behind his back. "I was lookin' for work," he says.

"Here we go." Geraldine's up and headed for the bench.

The judge pounds his gavel. "Mr. Holliston," he says, beckoning with one hand, "approach."

Judge Gould frowns at Geraldine while they wait for Holliston to join them. An objection was in order. "Here we go" wasn't.

The room grows noisy while the three of them huddle at the

side of the bench farthest from the jury. Sidebars always ratchet up the volume in the courtroom. Jurors don't like to be left out; spectators don't either. They're not missing much this time, though. No doubt the judge is instructing Derrick Holliston on the ABCs of opening statement; teaching him that the word *I* doesn't belong in the room right now; informing him that the only way he gets to tell the jurors he was looking for work is by taking the witness stand. They've already heard that particular tidbit, though. It can't be taken back.

Harry clears his throat and leans close to me, his eyes on the trio at the bench, his expression almost amused. "This little development is going to wreak havoc with the game plan," he says.

He's right, of course. The game plan calls for two days of witness testimony, less if the defendant doesn't testify. At that point, the jurors will be sequestered until they return their verdict. And though no one can predict how long deliberations will take in any case, Judge Gould fully anticipated sending them all home in plenty of time to decorate for Christmas. That's open to question now.

"What do you think?" I ask Harry. "New Year's Eve?"

He shakes his head, his hazel eyes on Holliston's back. "Nope. I'm thinking little pink hearts."

The judge wraps up his instructions and directs the defendant back toward the jury box. Holliston looks smug when he turns; he seems certain he just digested three years of law school in six minutes. He'll probably expect his sheepskin by the end of the day.

Geraldine shakes her blond bangs as she returns to her table and takes her seat next to Clarence. She's disgusted.

Harry pulls a yellow legal pad from his schoolbag and draws three hearts on it, an elaborate arrow piercing each one.

"It's like the boss lady said," Holliston tells the panel, pointing back at Geraldine. "You'll hear it from the cop."

Geraldine turns and looks at Harry and me, then rolls her green eyes to the ceiling. She's flattered to be incorporated into our ex-client's opening, she telegraphs. And she's downright delighted to be known as "the boss lady."

"Not just any cop," Holliston continues. "The top dawg. He'll tell you what went down that night. He'll tell you all about it."

Geraldine stands, anticipating the pretend lawyer's next transgression. Judge Gould fires a silent warning at her. We're getting nowhere fast here, and Holliston hasn't crossed the line this time. Not yet, anyhow.

"He'll tell you that priest hit on me."

So much for not crossing the line.

"He'll tell them no such thing!" Geraldine's chair topples backward and Clarence catches it. She's halfway to the bench, both hands in the air.

The gavel descends.

Harry draws a line through his artwork. "Faith and begorra," he says. His brogue is atrocious. "We'd best push our finish date back a wee bit." He moves his legal pad closer to me as he replaces each heart with a shamrock.

"Move for an instruction, Your Honor." Geraldine is in front of the bench now and she's livid. She'll get her instruction, but Judge Gould waves Holliston over for another sidebar tutorial first.

The judge stands, moves to the far side of his bench again, and delivers another lecture. He's far more animated this time, though. He points his index finger at Holliston's chest repeatedly as he reiterates the ground rules. He listens to a comment from Geraldine, nodding, and then shoos both of them away. It's obvious he's every bit as frustrated as Geraldine is. Holliston is entirely unruffled; he seems to think his opening statement is proceeding quite smoothly.

Harry leans closer. "Ix-nay on dear Saint Paddy," he says, his brogue even worse when he mixes it with pig Latin. "It pains me to say it, Colleen, but I'm thinking marshmallow peeps."

"Colleen" takes his pen away before he can draw them.

"Ladies and gentlemen," Judge Gould intones, "you will disregard Mr. Holliston's last comment."

They nod in unison.

"Mr. Holliston," the judge sighs, "you may proceed."

Holliston moves closer to the box.

"As we discussed," the judge adds.

"Okay, now," Holliston says, his tone suggesting he's about had it with these silly interruptions, "like I was sayin', the top cop is gonna tell you what I told him. And I told him the truth."

"Your Honor!" Geraldine doesn't even bother to stand this time.

"Mr. Holliston!" Judge Gould sounds like he's at the end of his rope. "If I hear the word *I* once more, sir, you will take your seat."

"Okay, okay." Holliston is annoyed. He shakes his head at the jurors. "The cop's gonna tell you five things."

He raises his hand and holds up one finger, à la Geraldine. "First," he says, "that priest hit on me. And I mean big-time."

"There he goes again," Geraldine announces.

"Mr. Holliston," the judge warns.

Gregory Harmon folds his arms across his chest. Cora Rowlands knits her brow. The others don't move.

"So I say to him, I say, you know, I ain't that way." Holliston holds up his other hand and flutters it, just in case any of the jurors don't know what *that way* means.

Geraldine drops her head back against her chair and stares at the ceiling.

"Mr. Holliston," Judge Gould repeats, his tone menacing now.

Maria Marzetti plants her elbow on an armrest, cups her chin in her palm. Her back-row admirer stares again, making no effort to mask his interest.

"But the priest don't like that," Holliston says. "He ain't takin' no for an answer. He starts gettin' rough. And I mean *real* rough, serious rough."

Judge Gould looks skyward, praying for patience, maybe, and takes his glasses off.

Holliston stares at his solitary raised finger as if he'd forgotten it was there. "Okay," he says, adding two more, "so that's three. He hits on me; I say no way; he goes wacko."

Geraldine gets to her feet. "Your Honor. Please."

"Mr. Holliston, remember the litany." Judge Gould massages the bridge of his nose, then puts his glasses back on.

Holliston wheels around and gapes at the bench, looking like he can't figure out why the judge is still sitting there. "Oh," he says, "that." He stares out at the crowded gallery for a moment and shakes his head sadly, his expression saying this judge is being unnecessarily difficult—and everyone in the room surely knows it. "Okay," he says, turning back to the jurors, "so the cop is gonna tell you all these things is what I told him."

He pauses and turns to look up at the bench again, his raised eyebrows asking: *Satisfied now?*

"Move on, sir," the judge says.

He resumes his finger count. "So then," he says, adding the fourth, "I defend myself. I mean, what guy in his right mind ain't gonna defend himself against *that*, right?"

I can think of dozens of adjectives to describe Derrick Holliston. Right-minded isn't one of them.

Geraldine doesn't bother getting up; she flings both arms in the air.

"Mr. Holliston," the judge says yet again.

"Wish we'd brought popcorn," Harry whispers. "This is Oscar material."

"Only if Hollywood creates a Most Painful Performance category," I tell him.

Holliston doesn't even turn around for the judge's latest admonition. "Okay," he says to the jurors, "the cop is gonna tell you I *told* him I was defendin' myself." He adds his thumb to his finger lineup and stares at it for a moment before he continues. "And he's gonna tell you I grabbed for somethin'—dint matter what—to fight the guy off with. There was some kinda toolbox there—on the counter—and I grabbed the first thing I could out of it. Turns out it was some kinda pick, a long, pointy thing. I dint even see it till everything was over."

"Your Honor." Geraldine's up again.

"What?" Holliston asks her. "I told the cop that. He had his tape recorder goin'. Plus he wrote it down. I watched him."

Judge Gould bangs his gavel. "You'll direct your comments to the court, sir. No one else."

Holliston looks up at the bench and shrugs. Doesn't matter to him, it seems.

The judge takes a deep breath and exhales slowly. "Move on, sir," he says yet again.

Geraldine turns and stares at Harry and me before she sits. She wants the jurors to do likewise, wants to remind them we're here, wants them to be fully aware that all of this is unnecessary. It works. Most of them look our way before they return their attention to Holliston.

"So listen to that cop," he tells them. "You don't need to listen to nobody else, as far as I'm concerned. Nobody else got anything to say that matters."

I expect Geraldine to jump up again—Holliston's way out of line—but she doesn't. Instead, she leans back in her chair and crosses her lean legs, one spiked heel dangling above the thick carpet. She's relaxed. I'm confused.

"Uh-oh," Harry says, and my confusion evaporates. He's right. Geraldine is happy with these particular inappropriate comments. We'll probably hear them again—next time from her.

"That cop," Holliston says as he backs up to his table, "he's the only guy you need to listen to. He's gonna tell you the truth."

Judge Gould stares down at Geraldine, obviously waiting for her to explode.

She doesn't.

CHAPTER 15

"I figure this guy can take it from here," Holliston says, jerking his neatly groomed head back toward Harry.

We're in chambers, once again listening to the defendant dictate the procedural details of his murder trial. He's reversed his position, decided he wants representation after all. He announced his change of heart to the entire courtroom as soon as Geraldine called her first witness. Judge Gould immediately declared a recess, excused the jurors, and ordered the attorneys—even the faux attorney—into chambers.

The judge isn't happy. "Mr. Holliston," he says, "this isn't a game."

"You got that right." Once again, Derrick Holliston is the only person in the room who's seated. He's slouched in one of the two chairs facing the judge's desk, a slight smile on his face, his fingers drumming the armrests. He looks around at each of us—even his armed chaperones—pleased that we showed up on time for his staff meeting.

Geraldine's been pacing since we came in here, as usual, but she stops short in front of Holliston now and glares down at him, her green eyes aglow. "You're not going to take the stand, are you?"

Harry's between the two of them before I realize he's moved from his spot against the wall beside me. "Whoa, sister," he says, his open palm almost touching Holliston's face. "You don't get that information now."

Massachusetts attorneys adhere to an archaic tradition of referring to each other as "Brother Counsel" or "Sister Counsel." Even so, Harry makes Geraldine crazy when he calls her plain old "sister." He also makes her crazy when he's right. And he's right now. She's doesn't get that information yet. A criminal defendant can decide to testify—or not—at any time before the defense rests. If the decision is made sooner rather than later—and it almost always is—the prosecutor isn't privy to it. Far better to keep her in the dark until the last moment.

She wheels around to face the judge, her eyes on fire now. "Do you see what's going on here?"

He does. We all do. Holliston has *already* testified. He told the jurors his story without taking the stand—without submitting to an oath, without facing cross-examination, and without risking the admission of his prior attack on the Butcher. Harry was right. *Crazy like a fox.*

Judge Gould nods at Geraldine, leans on the top of his chair, and tosses his glasses on the desk. "Mr. Holliston," he says, "how many times do you intend to change your mind on this issue during the course of trial?"

Holliston takes a few moments to mull it over. "Prob'ly not again," he says, rubbing his clean-shaven chin. "Like I said"—he looks over at Harry and sneers—"the rest of this shouldn't be that hard, so I think he'll be okay from here."

Harry laughs at the backhanded endorsement.

"But I'll level with you," Holliston continues. He leans toward the judge, ready to share a long-held confidence with a trusted colleague. "I'd just as soon get a new lawyer. I ain't seen much spark out of this one so far."

Judge Gould shakes his head before the complaint is complete. "Not going to happen, Mr. Holliston. Mr. Madigan is your court-appointed defender. He'll provide you with as thorough a defense to these allegations as any attorney in the county could deliver—if you let him."

Holliston sits up straighter and slaps his knees, his grin suggesting the judge just delivered one hell of a punch line. "That's good," he says. "That's real good." Both guards move closer to his chair.

The judge ignores him, looks at Harry instead. "You're ready, Mr. Madigan?"

Harry nods.

Judge Gould sighs and looks around the room at all of us as he retrieves his glasses and heads for the door. "All right, then," he says. "Let's get on with it."

Holliston jumps up, nodding; he thinks that's a swell idea.

The judge exits chambers first and Big Red calls the courtroom to its collective feet. Holliston and his escorts follow, Geraldine and Clarence close behind. Geraldine pauses before the doorway, though, and directs Clarence out first. She turns back to Harry, frowning, and shakes her blond head. "I hope I don't live long enough to have to say these words again," she tells him, "but I'm damn glad you're back on board."

CHAPTER 16

Calvin Ramsey is all business; he always is. His direct testimony went by the book. Ivy League educational background, stellar employment history, and impressive professional affiliations filled the first twenty minutes or so. Details of his current responsibilities as Barnstable County's Medical Examiner took the next fifteen. Testimony specific to this case filled a solid hour.

The doctor's direct included the introduction of five black-and-white photographs, all taken during the autopsy he performed almost a year ago, on the day after Christmas. Each shows a puncture wound, or a combination of puncture wounds, on Francis Patrick McMahon's body. Most of the jurors looked disturbed as the graphic images circulated among them. Robert Eastman glanced over at Alex Doane and shook his head sadly.

Maria Marzetti pressed a fist to her mouth. Cora Rowlands shuddered.

Under Geraldine's careful questioning, Dr. Ramsey tied Derrick Holliston to the dead man in no uncertain terms. Prints, hair follicles—even fibers from Holliston's jacket and jeans—all combine to leave little doubt as to who paid an unexpected visit to St. Veronica's sacristy last Christmas Eve. An airtight ID, unless our client suddenly decides to claim he has an identical twin in the neighborhood who shares his wardrobe. Technically, of course, the identification evidence wasn't necessary. Holliston's self-defense claim admits as much. Still, our District Attorney isn't taking any chances; she intends to prove every element of the crime, contested or not.

The Medical Examiner's direct ended with the crux of the matter: the deceased sustained eight puncture wounds in all. Five would have been non-life-threatening, had they been treated in time. The abdominal wounds—even if medically attended promptly—may or may not have proved fatal. It remains an open question. The aortal puncture, of course, is anything but. It cinched the priest's fate instantly. "That one," Calvin Ramsey said, pointing to the top photograph in the stack on the jury box railing in response to Geraldine's final question. "The entry wound is tiny," he told the attentive jurors, "as they all are, but that one was fatal. Father McMahon expired within minutes of this puncture being inflicted."

The fourteen faces in the box are somber. More than a few look a little bit sick. And now it's Harry's turn, whether he likes it or not. He scoops all five photographs from the jury box railing and returns them to Geraldine's table, facedown, before he speaks. "Dr. Ramsey," he says as he walks toward the witness box, "you're aware, are you not, sir, that Mr. Holliston has entered a self-defense claim?"

"I am."

"So you're aware he admits stabbing the deceased?"

"Yes."

"Yet you went to great lengths here today to prove it."

Dr. Ramsey actually smiles at Harry. "I answer the questions, Mr. Madigan. I don't choose them."

Touché.

Harry's not surprised by the doctor's response; he knew it was coming. But he's got precious little to work with in this case. He needs to raise every issue he can—even the ones that bite back—so he'll have at least some material he can weave into a credible closing argument. He turns and stares at Geraldine Schilling, the person who *does* choose the questions, and waits until the jurors do too. "Were any of the deceased's wounds inflicted from behind?" he says at last.

The witness tilts his head to one side. "From behind? No, certainly not." He gestures toward Geraldine's table, toward the upside-down photographs, suggesting maybe Harry hasn't seen them yet. "The puncture wounds are all on the front of the body," he says.

Harry nods repeatedly, as if this fact is particularly meaningful. It's not, but he'll make something of it; he has to. "Mr. Holliston and the deceased were face-to-face, then," he says, "when the altercation occurred. Is that correct, Doctor?"

Geraldine stirs but she doesn't object. Harry's on the brink of impropriety, teetering on the edge of it, but he hasn't quite crossed the line.

"I would assume so," the witness answers. He seems hesitant, though. He loosens his tie, looking uncomfortable. Maybe it's the word *altercation*.

Geraldine half stands, ready for battle, in case Harry plans to take this line of questioning any further. Even she knows she shouldn't bother, though. She's tried enough cases against Harry Madigan to know he won't. He's gotten as much as he can get from this witness; trying to squeeze out more would be stupid. At best, it would get us nowhere. At worst, it would alienate the jury. It's too easy for a lawyer to look like a shark when the witness being crossed is as professional, as straightforward, as this one.

Harry walks back toward our table, his eyes on the floor. He's running through a mental checklist, no doubt, making sure he hasn't overlooked any detail before he dismisses the Medical Examiner. He hasn't. At this point, he has enough to argue in closing that the Commonwealth's theory of the case doesn't make any sense, that our client would have attacked from behind had he planned a robbery/murder, that a face-to-face confrontation is far more consistent with Holliston's version of events. He turns back to face the witness when he reaches our table. "Thank you, Dr. Ramsey," he says. "Nothing further."

Judge Gould tells the doctor he's free to go. Geraldine's on her feet, in front of the bench, looking anxious to call her next witness. Harry takes his seat and Holliston leans so far forward on the other side of me his ear almost touches the table. "What?" he says to Harry, his hands spread wide. "That's all you got?"

Holliston was hoping for a Johnnie Cochran performance, it seems. And Harry would have delivered one, gladly, were it not for one problem: the facts.

Harry stares back at Holliston and, for the first time that I've seen, his eyes reveal the depth of his disdain for our court-imposed client. "Nope," he says evenly after a pause. "That's not all I got. But it's sure as hell all *you* got."

Judge Gould looks down at our eager District Attorney and then checks the pendulum clock. It's one-fifteen. He announces the midday break almost apologetically; he knows Geraldine would rather steamroll ahead. She returns to her table shaking her head; she never has understood this daily ritual called lunch.

The judge instructs the jurors not to discuss the case, not even among themselves, until they begin formal deliberations. He tells the lawyers to be back and ready to roll no later than two-thirty. When he stands, we all follow suit and watch as he disappears into chambers on the double.

Big Red leads the jurors out the side door. As soon as it shuts behind them, one of the prison guards slaps the hardware on Holliston and points him toward lockup. He looks over his shoulder and sneers at us as he leaves. "You heard the man," he says to Harry. "Make sure you get back here on time. Two-thirty sharp."

Harry doesn't let on he hears, doesn't even look in Holliston's direction. We grab our heavy coats and head for the side exit without a word. It's Piccadilly Deli time again, but Harry promised we'd make it quick today; even said he'd pass on the pie, if necessary. Chatham's Chief of Police is Geraldine's next witness. He's mine to cross. And—Holliston's high hopes notwithstanding—my gut says the Chief will be our biggest problem.

CHAPTER 17

The Kydd isn't answering the phones—not the office line and not his cell. I've gotten our automated message service three times, talked to it twice. Now I'm listening to the Kydd's personal recording, telling me in Southern-speak to wait for the beep before leaving my message on his cell phone. I obey, ask him to call me as soon as he can, and then give up and join Harry at our usual table near the front windows. They're fogged, trapped between the steamy sauna of the deli and the arctic temperatures outside.

"Where the hell is he?" I don't expect Harry to know; I'm just thinking out loud.

"Maybe he's doing what we're doing," Harry suggests after he swallows. "Or what one of us is doing." He toasts me with his chocolate milk. "Lunch."

I sip my coffee and shake my head; that explanation doesn't fit. Much as he hates his "secretarial duties," as he calls them, the Kydd takes his office obligations seriously. He wouldn't leave the place unmanned for the sake of food; he'd order in. If he's not there—and it's pretty clear he's not—something important has called him away. My stomach churns as my brain replays yesterday's confession from Senator Kendrick. *They'll get to me sooner, not later. . . . We were together Thursday night, the night before she disappeared. . . . But I kept thinking we'd hear from Michelle. . . . I just didn't think anything bad had happened to her. But now I'm afraid I was wrong.*

"Besides," Harry continues, finishing off the first half of his foot-long sub, "the Kydd's about had it with telephones. And who the hell can blame him? If I were in his shoes, I'd hurl them all into Nantucket Sound."

Today my partner's luncheon selection is a Philly-style steak and cheese, smothered with sautéed onions and dripping jalapeño sauce—a little something easy on the stomach. "I don't think so," I tell him. "I don't think the Kydd would leave the office and shut down his cell just because he's sick of taking calls. Something's up."

Harry shrugs, lobs his empty chocolate milk carton into the trash bin, and opens a second quart. "If so, the Kydd will handle it. And if he can't, he'll call. He's got a good head on his shoulders."

That's true. Still, I find the Kydd's absence unsettling. He always covers the office when we're in court. He's never gone AWOL before.

"You're worried about Chuck, aren't you?" Harry asks. I filled him in on Charles Kendrick's most recent revelations on the way to the courthouse this morning.

"You bet I am," I answer. "*Chuck* needs serious damage control. Even the best-case scenario leaves him in a world of hurt."

Harry stares across the table at me, his expression somber. We both know where the worst-case scenario leaves the senior senator.

We're quiet while Harry polishes off the second half of his midday meal, and I'm relieved when the last of it disappears. I'm anxious to get back. It's not that I'm ill prepared for this afternoon's tasks. I'm as ready as any defense lawyer can be. Even so, I want to go over my notes once more in the relative quiet of the courtroom. I want to review Tommy Fitzpatrick's report for the hundredth time. And I want to collect my thoughts before I face Chatham's Chief of Police, a credible witness if ever there was one.

I drain my cardboard coffee cup and reach for my coat, but the look on Harry's face stops me short. His hazel eyes focus on something over my shoulder, then light up as he crumples his napkins and balls up his butcher paper. He nods emphatically, does it again five seconds later. Pie, no doubt. With ice cream. We're not going anywhere any time soon.

"Pecan," he explains. His expression says we both understand the gravity of the situation now. He has no choice; he's powerless in the face of the mighty pecan.

I check my watch and head to the coffee station for another half cup, telling myself to chill. We have plenty of time, really; it's two-ten, and the deli is just a stone's throw from the courthouse. My cell phone sings as I reach for the pot—Luke constantly replaces its standard ring with electronic renditions of the most unlikely musical scores. Last week it was the theme from *Gilligan's Island*. The current selection is the William Tell Overture. Neither is a piece I would have chosen, but I don't get a vote.

I pour quickly, then pull the phone from my jacket pocket and breathe a sigh of relief when the incoming number lights up. "Kydd," I answer, "you had us worried."

The Kydd knows Harry and me well enough to know *I* was the only one worried. "Marty," he says, "where are you?"

I laugh as I head back to the table with my refill. "Funny, I was about to ask you the same question."

Harry's digging in, creamy vanilla ice cream already melting over his dark brown pie. The rapture on his face tells me it's Häagen-Dazs.

"Seriously," the Kydd says. "Where?"

"At the Piccadilly. Where else would we be in the middle of a trial day? And where the hell are you? I've been trying to reach you for almost an hour."

"Listen," he says. "I need to make this quick. The reception here is iffy. I'm too close to the water."

"Where the hell are you?" I repeat. "It's fifteen degrees outside, for God's sake. Hell of a day to take a stroll on the beach."

"I'm not *strolling*," he says through a flurry of static. "Trust me on that." He takes a deep breath and I wait. "I came here to meet a team from the ME's office," he says. "Smithy Stewart gave me a heads-up."

I set my cup down and then freeze beside our table, unable to sit. Smithy Stewart has been Chatham's harbormaster for decades. He doesn't ordinarily deal with the folks from the ME's office.

The Kydd stays quiet until the line clears. "I called as soon as I could," he says. "They just left."

Not only am I able to sit now; I need to. "With a corpse," I say as I drop into the chair across from Harry. My comment makes him set his fork down. It makes the elderly couple at the next table nervous. They gape at each other, then at me, then at each other again.

"That's right," the Kydd says. "Smithy spotted it during routine patrol this morning. In Pleasant Bay, floating toward shore with the incoming tide."

"Incoming tide," I repeat. Smithy doesn't ordinarily deal with floating bodies, either. Harry leans toward me. The elderly man and woman collect their belongings and move to a different table.

"Kydd," I ask for the third time, "where the hell are you?"

"Smithy brought the body to the nearest town landing," he says. "We all met him here. At Cow Yard."

Cow Yard. Off Old Harbor Road. A quarter mile from the Kendrick estate.

I force myself to breathe. "And?" I ask the Kydd. I'm pretty sure I know what's coming, though.

"On the record," he says, "nothing. Not a single comment for the press yet."

Our line is noisy again, but I can still understand him. "And off the record?" I ask.

The Kydd takes a deep breath. "Caucasian female," he says as he exhales. "Between twenty and thirty. Shoulder-length hair. Black."

I press against the high-backed chair and close my eyes, my mind unwillingly traveling to the Forresters' wraparound porch in Stamford. I try hard not to imagine the knock on the front door that will rouse first Catherine, and then Warren, from their well-worn family-room chairs. I try even harder not to picture their faces as they struggle to comprehend the hushed words delivered by some unlucky Connecticut cop. And I battle against the image of Catherine picking up the kitchen telephone, dialing Meredith's number, and telling her that the world—the one that's been spinning wildly for the past six days—has just come to an abrupt end.

The line is suddenly clear. "Marty," the Kydd says.

"I'm here," I tell him.

"Smithy recognized her from the news," he says. "It's Michelle."

Chapter 18

∭

Tommy Fitzpatrick is a cop's cop. Tall and broad-shouldered, with a full head of strawberry blond hair going pale—but not gray—as he ages, he's a commanding presence in any room. The courtroom is no exception. He's in full dress blues, entirely at ease in the witness box, his hat resting on the railing, his written report in his lap. He speaks directly to the jurors as he answers Geraldine's questions, as if he's known each member of the panel all his life. He's been Chatham's Chief for one decade, he tells them, on the force just shy of three. He'll mark his thirtieth anniversary in June, and he'll retire at the end of that month. He plans to work on his less-than-stellar golf game, explore Ireland with his wife of twenty-eight years, and spend a lot more time sport-fishing with their four grandchildren.

Harry turns to me, his eyebrows arched. Neither of us saw the gold watch on the horizon. And from where we sit, it's not a welcome prospect. Tommy Fitzpatrick plays by the rules, runs a clean department. Not all of them do.

Geraldine half sits on the edge of her table, digging a spiked heel into its leg, while the Chief chats comfortably with the jurors. She's trying to be patient, doing her best not to rush the preliminaries. She wants these jurors to like Tommy Fitzpatrick, after all, to trust him. He's a critical prosecution witness. Even so, patience doesn't come easily to Geraldine Schilling. She's fidgeting, dying to get to the good stuff.

The Chief pauses for a sip of water and Geraldine bolts from her table as if fired from a cannon. She carries two small stacks of eight-by-ten glossies to the witness box and sets them on the railing. Harry pulls our copies—a half dozen in all—from his schoolbag. They're shots taken by the crime scene photographer in St. Veronica's sacristy last Christmas Eve. Unlike the autopsy photos introduced this morning, these are in vivid color. And they're coming into evidence. Every last one of them.

During pretrial motions, Geraldine pushed hard for a jury "view": a field trip, of sorts, to the crime scene. While Judge Gould deemed a view unnecessary, he allowed Geraldine substantial leeway to introduce photographs of the scene instead. Of the dozen she proffered, half are coming in. And they're not pretty.

Harry spreads our copies across the table so we can follow along as Geraldine recites the necessary litany for each. *Were you present when this photograph was taken?* she asks the Chief. *Was it taken pursuant to your order and under your supervision? Does it accurately depict St. Veronica's sacristy as it appeared on the night in question?*

The Chief delivers the requisite number of affirmatives for each glossy and Geraldine moves the Court for permission to "publish" the first—yet another archaic term our bar association clings to. She wants to give it to the jurors, tell them to pass it around. Judge Gould nods his assent and Geraldine hands the first glossy to Gregory Harmon. He doesn't flinch when he takes it, but Cora Rowlands does. She looks sideways over his shoulder, erect in her chair, both hands pressed to her mouth.

Crime-scene photographs tell the part of the story no witness can convey. Even when the victim of a violent crime survives and testifies, and even when that testimony is so powerful it brings the room to a standstill, its impact often pales when compared with that of the crime scene photos. Words are essential, of course. And so is forensic evidence. But pictures like this one change jurors' lives, shatter the foundations of their views of humanity.

Cora Rowlands's eyes fill immediately. She doesn't take the glossy when Gregory Harmon offers it, instead signals for him to pass it to the juror on her left. She doesn't touch it, doesn't even look down when Harmon reaches across to hand it to her neighbor. She gazes up at the ceiling for a moment, then takes her glasses off and cleans them with a lace handkerchief. No doubt she hopes to erase the unwanted image from her mind's eye while she's at it. She can't, of course, not now and not any time soon. I feel a twinge of sympathy for her. At times, our system demands extraordinary efforts from ordinary citizens. This is one of them.

Geraldine takes a glossy from the second stack—a duplicate of the one being circulated in the jury box—and hands it to the Chief, asks him to identify it.

"This is the sacristy as we found it," he says, "when we first arrived on the scene, before anything was touched."

Harry pulls our copy to the edge of the table. Francis Patrick

McMahon is sprawled on the gray slate floor, his black cassock twisted and soaked in a sea of blood. His head is pointed toward a corner of the room and his eyes are open, his frameless glasses a few feet away on the floor, one lens shattered. His face, though uncut, bears half a dozen maroon blood blotches. And the white plaster walls on both sides of him are blood-spattered too. The body of an average-size adult holds about ten pints of blood; this photo makes it seem more like ten gallons.

Geraldine asks Tommy Fitzpatrick to walk the jurors through each of the remaining photos and she publishes each one to the panel as he does. The next four are close-ups of Father McMahon's wounds, most notably the fatal puncture to the aorta, the one we viewed in black and white with Dr. Ramsey. These photos aren't pleasant for the jurors to absorb, but they're not nearly as difficult as the first one was. These are anonymous body parts. The first was a whole human being.

Harry pulls each of our copies forward on the table as the Chief explains it, making a neat stack near the edge. He and I have examined all of these photographs many times, but we study each one again as the Chief testifies, then scan the members of the panel for their reactions. Holliston folds his arms and turns away from us, toward the side door, looking like he doesn't want to stick around for much more of this.

The last shot, number six, is different from the others. It's a photograph of an empty wicker basket, sitting on the sacristy's tidy counter. The jurors' relief is palpable as they pass it around. They've all seen enough gore for one day. Cora Rowlands has seen enough for a lifetime.

"And finally," Geraldine says to the Chief, "would you explain to the jurors the significance of this shot."

He nods and takes another sip of water. "We went back for that one," he says, "after we interviewed the pastor."

"Why was that?" Geraldine says. The question isn't necessary, though. The Chief's a seasoned witness; he doesn't need the minor prompts.

"The pastor was the first person on the scene," he says. "Monsignor Davis found the body. After he called us, he noticed the basket. He told us it shouldn't have been empty; it should have held the Christmas Vigil collection."

Holliston leans uncomfortably close to me. "Ain't you supposed to jump up right about now?" he says. "You ever hearda hearsay?"

He's getting in touch with his inner lawyer again. I shake my head at him, wishing he'd shut up and let me do my job.

"You even watch TV?" he says. "Christ, anybody who watches TV knows hearsay ain't allowed."

"Be quiet," I tell him. "Now."

He's wrong. Hearsay is only hearsay if the person being quoted is unavailable to testify, unavailable to be cross-examined. St. Veronica's pastor, Monsignor Dominic Davis, isn't; he's sitting in the hallway. He's Geraldine's next witness and, like all witnesses in serious cases, he's sequestered—excluded from the courtroom—until he testifies. I've neither the time nor the interest to explain any of this to Holliston, though. Besides, he's busy contorting his face and sighing over my gross incompetence.

"So the collection money was stolen?" Geraldine continues.

"Well, it was missing." Tommy Fitzpatrick is a careful witness; he avoids assumptions at all costs.

"Has it ever been recovered?" she asks.

"Not yet," he says. "So far we haven't found anything that was taken that night."

Something about that answer bothers me. I'm on my feet before my brain knows why. "Hold it," I say.

"Hold it?" Judge Gould echoes, and I can't blame him. That's not my usual mode of objecting—or anyone else's, for that matter.

My pulse is racing, but my mind is way ahead now. "Move to voir dire the witness, Your Honor."

"What?" Geraldine pivots to face me, plants her hands on her hips. "My Sister Counsel can't voir dire this witness. She can wait her turn, ask whatever burning questions she has on cross."

"These questions need to be asked now," I say, "while we're discussing these photographs." I'm in front of the bench, speaking directly to the judge.

"Ms. Nickerson," he says, his eyebrows knitting, "this is highly unusual."

A flurry of activity makes me turn. Geraldine is back at her table, exchanging hurried whispers with Clarence, rummaging through her file, confirming my hunch. Harry sees it too; it's plain on his face.

"I know it's unusual, Judge." I turn back to face him but he's not looking at me. He's watching the pair of panicked prosecutors instead. A quick scan of the room tells me everyone else is too.

"Your Honor," Geraldine says, "it seems my office may be guilty of a minor oversight. Perhaps we should take a short recess so we can rectify the matter."

"No recess," I say.

Judge Gould's eyes widen. Again, I can't blame him.

"Move to voir dire the witness," I repeat. "The motion's pending."

The judge is quiet for a moment, his eyes moving from me back to Geraldine. "I'll allow it," he says at last.

I pounce before the District Attorney can argue further. " 'So far we haven't found anything that was taken that night.' That was your answer to the prior question, was it not, Chief?"

He looks surprised, but not worried. Tommy Fitzpatrick is a straight shooter. He doesn't know what the hell's going on here—I'm not entirely sure I do, either—but he'll answer the questions put to him. And he'll answer them honestly, no matter who is asking. "Yes," he says. "That was my answer."

"Tell us specifically, Chief, what it is you haven't found."

He shrugs. "Like I said, we haven't found anything. Everything that was taken from the church that night is still missing."

"We're not just talking about money, are we?"

He looks over at Geraldine and a glimmer of understanding comes to his eyes. I don't have to turn around to know she looks sick. "No," he says. "We're not."

"What else was taken from St. Veronica's Chapel that night, Chief?"

He takes his glasses from an inside pocket and puts them on, then opens his written report and skims through it. "A monstrance," he says, tapping the page. "I have a devil of a time remembering that word."

"Tell the jurors what a monstrance *is*, will you, Chief?" He'll be broadening my vocabulary as well, but I try not to let on.

"I had to ask the pastor the same question," he says, as if reading my mind. "And I was raised Catholic."

A few of the jurors chuckle.

"It's a solid-gold stand," he says, "used to hold the host when it's exposed on the altar for any length of time. The host is inserted into a small window at the top, so it can be viewed by the visiting faithful, but not touched. Until fairly recently, only an ordained priest was permitted to touch the host."

"Is the monstrance valuable?" I ask.

He shrugs again. "It's gold," he says. "The thief would find a taker if he melted it down, I suppose."

"And you're certain it was taken from the chapel the night Francis McMahon was killed?"

"The pastor is," the Chief says. "Monsignor Davis said the monstrance was to be on display from the end of the Vigil Mass until midnight, the chapel unlocked so parishioners could enjoy private visitation."

I turn to the defense table, where our client has both arms flung outward, his eyes raised to the heavens. He's apparently disgusted once again with my failure to invoke the TV version of the hearsay rule. He has no idea what a lucky break he's about to get. It should happen to a nicer guy.

I check in with Harry and he gives me the go-ahead nod; we're on the same page. I wait, though, until the room falls silent. I want to say it quietly, calmly. "We move for a mistrial, Your Honor, on the grounds of prosecutorial misconduct."

The place erupts.

Reporters head for the double doors, many of them running backward so as not to miss anything on the way out. Judge Gould bangs his gavel repeatedly, then signals Big Red to get the jurors the hell out of here. He jumps up and descends from the bench as they file through the side door, his steps heavy, his robe billowing as he strides. "Counsel," he says, heading for chambers, "inside. Now."

Our client gets to his feet at once and Judge Gould wheels around to face him. "I called for counsel, Mr. Holliston," the judge says. He's winded, obviously exasperated. "Believe it or not, sir, that does *not* include you."

The defendant drops back into his chair, shaking his head. His expression says he's certain this situation is far beyond anything Harry and I can handle.

We follow the judge into chambers, Geraldine and Clarence behind us. Geraldine's on the defensive even before her sidekick shuts the door. "It was an oversight," she says, "nothing more than that."

Harry actually laughs. "I hope our District Attorney won't take offense," he says to the judge, "but we see it differently."

Judge Gould eases into the chair at his desk and reaches under his robe to loosen his tie. "Ms. Schilling," he says, "this is not a matter the court takes lightly."

I slip into a seat in front of the desk and Geraldine perches on the edge of the chair next to mine. She's suddenly silent, a rare phenomenon.

"Assuming the best," the judge continues, "that it was an honest mistake, your office's failure to disclose the missing monstrance to the defense is a problem. A real one."

"We kept it quiet initially," Geraldine says, "as an investigative tool. Frankly, by the time we were preparing for trial, I'd forgotten all about it. We never intended to withhold its disappearance from the defense."

The judge shakes his head, looking like he's about to tell her that good intentions don't make a whit of difference, but Clarence pipes up first. "It's my fault," he says. "I dropped the ball."

He's leaning against the side wall and he's visibly distraught. He's also correct. This is the kind of omission he should have caught. It's his job to worry about the details—especially the technical ones—while Geraldine focuses on the big picture. He's a decent sort, Clarence, but as Harry's fond of saying, he's about two oysters shy of a bushel.

Harry feels sorry for Clarence now, though; I can see it in his eyes. We've all made plenty of mistakes in this heavily detailed business. And we all feel guilty as hell when we do. But in the early years, when you're new to the practice, each misstep seems like the end of the world.

Geraldine shuts Clarence down with one raised hand, not turning to look at him. She'll probably chew him up and spit him out later, in the privacy of her office, but she won't let him take the blame here. "Okay," she says to the judge. "My error. But what difference does it make? It's not as if Holliston ever claimed he *didn't* kill the priest. He admitted that much from the get-go. The missing monstrance doesn't change anything."

She's right. It doesn't. But as every criminal defense lawyer learns in the first week or so of practice, a prosecutorial error—even one that has no real bearing on the substance of the proceedings—is a rare gift. We'll milk it now, worry about whether it's worth anything later.

"You're wrong," Harry says to her. "It changes a lot. It's one more item that *wasn't* in Derrick Holliston's possession when he was picked up, one more item that *wasn't* found in his apartment—or anywhere else, for that matter—when he was taken into custody. It's one more piece of evidence that tends to prove his version of events, or—at the very least—*dis*prove yours."

He's good, Harry Madigan. If I didn't know better, I'd think he believes what he's saying.

Geraldine throws her hands in the air. "Go ahead," she says. "Take your mistrial." She checks her watch. "I'll refile before the day is out."

She's calling our bluff, of course. We don't really want a new trial and she knows it. We'll never get another opportunity like this one.

"We'll settle for an instruction," Harry says. His expression suggests he's less than satisfied with that solution, but everyone in the room knows he's not. This is a break few criminal defendants get. The judge will tell the jurors that the District Attorney's office misbehaved, failed to play by the rules. And from that moment on, our case will be about the DA's misconduct, not Holliston's.

"All right, then," the judge says as he stands, "let's get on with it. I'll give the instruction and we'll wrap it up with this witness. I'm sorry," he says to Geraldine from the doorway, "but you'll have to bring your pastor back tomorrow."

She nods, then follows him out of the room without a word. Rescheduling the pastor is the least of her problems at the moment. Clarence slinks out behind her. Harry and I follow.

Holliston's angry eyes bore into us as we approach the defense table, his glare saying he's certain we did a less than adequate job for him behind closed doors. "I dint take no monster," he says as soon as we sit. "I hope you told them people that."

Neither of us answers. Instead, we focus on Judge Gould, who's already settled on the bench, poised to give the instruction. "Ladies and gentlemen," he says to the panel, "it has come to the court's attention that certain material evidence known to the District Attorney's office has not heretofore been disclosed to the defense."

The jurors' gazes move from the judge to Geraldine. Their expressions are serious, concerned.

"In the Commonwealth of Massachusetts," Judge Gould continues, "the prosecuting attorney bears a burden of full disclosure. In other words, it is incumbent upon the prosecutor to disclose all material facts to the defendant and his lawyers prior to trial. In the case before us, the prosecutor failed to do so."

Again, the jurors turn their attention to Geraldine. She stares straight ahead.

"In particular," the judge says, "the District Attorney's office failed to inform the defense that an item of value, a solid gold monstrance, was taken from St. Veronica's Chapel on the night of Father McMahon's death."

Holliston bolts upright. He looks indignant.

"The prosecution's failure to disclose is particularly troubling when the evidence is exculpatory, as it is here. Like the collection proceeds, the monstrance has never been recovered. It was not in the defendant's possession at the time of his arrest. It has not been linked to him in any way."

The jurors' eyes move to our table now. I hope Holliston has his face under control, but I don't dare look.

"Our Supreme Judicial Court has recently held that judges should begin instructing juries in criminal trials to be 'skeptical' when either police officers or prosecutors fail to abide by the rules. The court also held we should instruct juries to weigh the Commonwealth's case 'with great care and caution' whenever proper procedures are not followed."

Holliston's timing couldn't be much better. The high court issued that ruling less than a year ago.

"Mr. Holliston is entitled to every reasonable inference you may draw from the missing monstrance. He's also entitled to every reasonable inference you may draw from the District Attorney's failure to disclose that fact."

With that, the judge faces front and stares at Geraldine. The jurors study her too, all of them, and more than a few look troubled.

Harry leans back in his chair and snaps a chewed-up pencil in two. "How many times in the past twenty-three years have I wished Geraldine Schilling would screw up?" he says. "Why the hell did she do it now?"

CHAPTER 19

The T intersection outside our 1840 farmhouse–turned–law office is the gateway to Chatham. Back roads into town exist, of course, but anyone wanting to stay on main thoroughfares will pass through this juncture en route to our charming village center. The antique Cape next to our building houses the Chatham Chamber of Commerce, where volunteers and merchants welcome weekly renters and day-trippers throughout the summer, recommending breakfast joints, fish markets, and seal-watch cruises; handing out menus, maps, and brochures. More than once each season, some confused out-of-towner wanders into our front office looking for directions to the Friday-night band concert. Harry patiently points every one of them toward the gazebo in Kate Gould Park, always with a plug for the PTA's cotton candy machine.

During the season, traffic is perpetually heavy here, both two-lane roads constantly clogged with carloads of tourists headed for beaches, shops, and restaurants. After Labor Day, the stream of visiting vehicles thins, the whole area growing markedly quieter overnight. By this time of year it's normally downright desolate, the roads clogged only with snowbanks left behind by the town's plows. Not today, though.

Today the waist-high white banks have company, and plenty of it. The Chamber of Commerce parking lot is full, though the building is closed until May. Cars and trucks that couldn't find space in that lot are strewn along both sides of our road, though no parking is allowed on either. Chatham cops are all over the place, slipping orange cardboard citations under icy windshield wipers, barking orders at those vehicle owners they can locate, and directing traffic impatiently while a solitary tow truck tries to make its way through the quagmire.

Our narrow driveway is filled to capacity, the Kydd's pickup and my Thunderbird hemmed in by two dark gray sedans I've never seen before. Harry pulls in behind them, then up onto the front lawn, and stops the Jeep next to Senator Kendrick's Hummer. "Oh, good," he says as he cuts the engine. "Company."

We collect our belongings, climb out of the Jeep, and Harry takes a leisurely stroll around the two mystery cars. He kneads his chin, his expression puzzled. The sedans are identical and they're impossibly clean, somehow immune to the slush, sand, and salt that coat every other vehicle in sight. "You have friends I don't know about?" he asks. "People who wash their cars?"

I don't answer.

Two men in dark overcoats pace in opposite directions on our small front porch, one with his hands jammed into his pockets, the other talking into his palm. I assume there's a phone in it. They glance at Harry and me as we approach, but both quickly return their focus to the noisy crowd on the sidewalk. It's multiplying by the minute, kept in check on the other side of our split-rail fence by a human barrier of Chatham police officers. I recognize a few faces in the assembly—members of the press for the most part—and they shout hurried questions at us as we cross the front lawn. Harry's name is called out more than once—and mine, too—but I can't decipher much else. Two TV vans idle in the Chamber of Commerce driveway, their lights and cameras pointed in our direction. It's after six; it should be pitch black out here now. But, thanks to the TV crews, it's not.

The talker snaps his miniature phone shut, drops it into his coat pocket, and plants himself at the top of the three brick steps leading up to the porch, his stance wide. "You Madigan?" he asks, pulling his black wool cap tight over his ears. His hatless partner joins him, outturned palm demanding: *Hold it right there.*

Harry pauses on the bottom step and laughs. "You boys are forgetting your manners," he says as he continues the short climb to the porch. "That's not how it's done in these United States of America."

He's nose to nose with the one in the black cap now, and neither of our visitors is happy about it. "You're supposed to tell *me* who *you* are," he says to both of them, "and you're supposed to prove it before you ask me a goddamned thing."

They stare at him, stoic.

Harry shifts his schoolbag from one gloved hand to the other and claps the black capped one on the shoulder. "You want me to recommend you for retraining?" he asks them both, his tone entirely sincere. "Or do you want to try that again?"

Both men scowl, but each one reaches into an inside pocket and pulls out a laminated ID. Harry takes his sweet time perusing both, his hand resting comfortably on Black Cap's shoulder while he reads. "Secret Service," he says to me at last. "We're safe now."

Secret Service. Of course. Senator Kendrick normally keeps a low profile when he's in Chatham. Now that Michelle's body has been recovered here, that won't be possible.

"We have another team out back," Hatless tells him.

Harry's still looking over his shoulder at me. "We're a veritable fortress," he says.

Black Cap removes Harry's hand from his shoulder, holding the glove with two fingers as if it's toxic. "You Madigan?" he tries again.

"One and the same," Harry answers, taking a gallant bow. "And may I present the lovely Miss Nickerson?" He sweeps one hand toward me, as though I'm the guest of honor at a debutante ball.

Hatless pulls a notepad from his pocket. "She's on here," he says to his partner, taking a pencil from behind his ear and tapping the eraser end of it against the page. "Nickerson, Martha."

Harry grins as I join the three of them on the porch. "Come, Nickerson Martha," he says, offering his arm. "I'm sure Jeeves has the martinis mixed."

The closest thing Harry and I have to a Jeeves, of course, is the Kydd. And I'm pretty sure he doesn't know how to mix a martini. Still, if he offered one, I wouldn't turn it down. A stiff drink sounds like a good idea at the moment. Two, maybe.

The front office is empty and the sounds of the TV tell us the Kydd and Charles Kendrick are in the conference room. Harry and I hang our heavy coats on the rack and then join them, but they barely look up when we enter. They're in side-by-side wing chairs, their eyes glued to the evening news. The Kydd's are glistening; he has a heart the size of Texas. The Senator's aren't, but the network of fine, pink lines around the whites of his gray-blues tell me he hasn't been dry-eyed for long. Michelle Forrester is the top story. The four of us watch in silence as two Coast Guardsmen lift a draped stretcher from Smithy's patrol boat and carry it to the county van waiting at Cow Yard.

Geraldine Schilling appears on the screen, looking the way she always looks on TV: like she just emerged from a two-week stint at a Beverly Hills spa. The autopsy is ongoing, she tells the horde assembled outside the Superior Courthouse. She expects to have the Medical Examiner's report in hand first thing tomorrow morning. She'll issue an update then. And she will, she assures her audience, bring the perpetrator of this heinous crime to justice. She turns her back to the crowd without another word and reenters the courthouse. The anchorwoman pauses for a station break. The Kydd hits the mute button.

Harry rests a hand on the Senator's shoulder, then drops into the chair beside him. "How're you holding up?" he asks.

Charles Kendrick shakes his head slowly, his eyes still glued to the glow of the television screen. He doesn't answer.

I unbutton my suit jacket and half-sit on the edge of the conference room table. We're going to be here for a while, it seems.

"Geraldine called," the Kydd says quietly. "She wants Senator Kendrick to come in tomorrow."

"That's out of the question." I realize too late that I've snapped at the Kydd, a classic shoot-the-messenger reaction.

He shrugs. "She said she'd see him at his convenience—before the Holliston trial resumes in the morning, or at the lunch break, or at the end of the day. She's hoping he'll do this voluntarily."

"She is not," Harry says. "She knows better."

"But shouldn't I? Shouldn't I at least *try* to help?" The Senator directs his query to Harry, but Harry turns to me. Charles Kendrick isn't going to like the answer to that question. I'm the one who should give it to him.

"No," I say. "You shouldn't."

"But—"

"Everything is changed now." I hold up both hands to cut him off, then point to the still-silent TV screen. "Michelle is dead. You can't help her. No one can."

His lips part, but he says nothing.

"Our District Attorney is an elected official," I tell him. "You don't need me to tell you this is a political nightmare. She wants an arrest yesterday. All you can do by talking now is hurt yourself."

The Senator's eyes move from mine to Harry's to the Kydd's. No doubt he's hoping one of them will contradict me, offer a kinder, gentler view of our system. No luck. He turns back to me, resigned. "All right," he says. "You tell me what to do. And I'll do it."

This is a first.

Charles Kendrick's gaze returns to the TV screen. The commercial break is over; coverage of the Michelle Forrester story has resumed.

"I loved her," he says to no one in particular.

And I believe him.

CHAPTER 20

It's almost nine by the time Harry and I pull up to my Windmill Lane cottage. A candy-apple Mustang is parked behind Luke's pickup in our newly shoveled driveway. Harry whistles and strolls around it as soon as we get out of the Jeep, and then he points out the Harvard bumper sticker. "Looks like your son has a visitor," he says, shaking his head. "Damn, that guy's doing something right."

"What does that mean?"

He shrugs. "You saw his heartthrob," he says. "And she drives *this* to boot."

I stare at him.

"This isn't one of the new ones," he tells me, examining the car again. "This baby is restored—vintage."

I'm feeling a bit vintage myself at the moment.

"I wonder if she has trouble getting parts," he adds.

I continue to stare. I'm not about to discuss Abby Kendrick's parts. Certainly not with Harry. He runs one gloved hand along the hood and chuckles. "That Luke," he says, "I've got to hand it to him. He's doing something right."

"So you mentioned."

Harry looks up all of a sudden, his eyes wide, as if he'd forgotten I was here until just now. "Of course," he says in a professorial tone, "I prefer a more *mature* woman myself."

"You're not helping your cause." I head for the back stairs.

"Preferably with a not-so-high-maintenance car," he says to my back.

"Give it up, Harry."

"With extremely high mileage," he calls after me.

"*Not* helping."

"And a low-to-the-ground chassis."

We're laughing uncontrollably by the time we spill through the kitchen door, more from fatigue than anything else. Harry pours a glass of Sancerre for me and opens a Heineken for himself, while I slice a loaf of French bread and take a wheel of Camembert and a bag of green grapes from the refrigerator. Not until we go into the living room do I realize it's dimly lit. My son has taken a stab at ambiance. A first, as far as I know.

A floor lamp in the far corner is on its lowest setting and two tapered candles flicker on the coffee table. The only other light in the room is the glow behind the glass doors of the woodstove. Abby Kendrick is seated on the couch, flanked by Luke and Danny Boy, and it's tough to tell which of them is more smitten. Danny Boy's tail wags when he sees me, thumps harder when Harry comes into the room, but he doesn't budge from Abby's side. "I'm going to remember this," Harry tells him, "the next time you want your ears scratched."

Luke flips on the light by the couch as soon as we join them. No need for ambiance now that Harry and I are here. I'm surprised he doesn't blow out the candles. "Harry," he says, "this is Abby Kendrick."

Harry shakes her hand. "Hello, Abby," he says. "We were just admiring your Mustang. It's a beauty."

I arch my eyebrows at him. He must be using the royal *we*.

"And you know my mom," Luke says to Abby.

"Yeah." She smiles at me as I set the fruit and cheese platter on the coffee table. "We met the other day."

Luke was surprised—and a little bit worried, I think—when I told him I'd met Abby on Tuesday morning. I'm pretty sure he was wondering if I'd said anything he should be embarrassed about, but he had the good sense to keep his concern to himself. "You two are in early," I say as I sink into one of the overstuffed chairs facing the couch.

"Yeah," Luke says, "we were thinking about watching a movie, but there's not much on." He picks up the remote and hits the power button, as if he needs to prove it. An acid reflux ad extinguishes what little ambiance was left in the room.

"You have trouble finding parts for that thing?" Harry asks Abby. He's a one-issue candidate sometimes.

She shakes her head. "My dad knows a guy in Southie," she says, "who services it for us. He never seems to have any trouble finding parts."

Southie is South Boston. If you know the right guy in Southie, you can get just about anything.

Abby looks like she has more to say on the matter of Mustang parts, but her eyes dart to the TV behind me and she stops talking. Harry and I both turn to see what's caught her eye. Bold print in the center of the screen says BREAKING NEWS: UPDATE ON THE HOUR. A banner at the top says BODY OF SENATE AIDE FOUND IN CAPE COD WATERS.

"On Cape Cod today," a familiar Boston anchorwoman says, "the body of Michelle Forrester, the Senate aide who's been missing since Thursday, was found in the shallows of Pleasant Bay, off the coast of Chatham. More at eleven."

"*Jesus,*" Luke says.

The color drains from Abby's face. "Did you know?" she asks me.

I nod. "We heard about it this afternoon."

"Does my father know?"

"Yes," I say. "He just left our office."

"How is he?"

"He's upset," I tell her honestly. "Like everyone else involved, he's extremely upset."

"I'm sorry," she says to Luke, "but I should go. My dad must be a mess."

She's right about that.

"And my mother," she adds. "Oh, God."

"Okay," Luke says. "Sure. I'll walk you out."

Harry and I are quiet as they put on their coats and head for the kitchen door. "That'll be interesting," Harry says as it shuts behind them.

"What will?"

"The dynamic in the Kendrick household tonight," he says. "You saw Chuck in the conference room. He's not going to be able to hide his pain, not even from his wife." He runs his hands through his tangled hair. "What in God's name does it feel like to watch your spouse grieve his dead lover?"

I shake my head at him. I hope I never know.

Danny Boy leaves the couch, trots across the room, and rests his grayish-red head on Harry's knees. "Oh, *now* you know who I am," Harry says. He's a pushover, though; he scratches Danny Boy's ears anyway.

"You know," Harry says, abandoning one ear long enough to point at the front window, toward the driveway, "if things work out here, you could land yourself some influential in-laws."

"Please," I say, "don't go there."

"Just think," he says to Danny Boy, "we could be eating our Thanksgiving dinners with a *senator's* family."

Danny Boy's tail thumps against the living room floor; he must be a Democrat. I hate to disappoint him, but my head hurts when I even *try* to imagine Thanksgiving dinner with Honey Kendrick. Coffee was complicated enough. "I don't think so," I tell Harry. "There's not enough Valium on the planet."

"Think we interrupted?" he asks, pointing toward the driveway again.

"Interrupted what?"

He doesn't answer; he just does the Groucho Marx thing with his eyebrows.

"Never mind," I tell him. "I'm sorry I asked."

The kitchen door slams and Luke appears in the living room doorway a few seconds later. He looks serious, worried even, but his eyes are bright, his cheeks flushed. And something tells me it's not just the winter wind that accounts for his high coloring. He points toward the road out front, toward the fading sound of Abby Kendrick's candy-apple coupe. "Is she great," he says eagerly, looking from Harry to me, "or what?"

CHAPTER 21

Friday, December 17

Monsignor Dominic Davis is in full Roman Catholic regalia—
Geraldine's brainchild, no doubt. I'm not a member of the flock,
but I've met enough priests in my day to know they don't *always*
sport ankle-length robes and pastel accessories. The Monsignor's
skullcap and waistband are a pinkish purple, and a matching sash
on his right side flows to the hem of his black linen cassock. I catch
Geraldine's eye and frown over the finery. A black suit with a simple Roman collar would have done the job.

Geraldine ignores me. She stands beside Monsignor Davis and
beams at him as he raises his right hand, places his left on the Holy
Bible, and takes the oath. "Your Eminence," she says as he sits,
"please state your full name and occupation for the record."

Harry turns to me, his hazel eyes as wide as they get, as the priest introduces himself to the jurors. "Your *what*?" he whispers.

"Don't look at me," I tell him. "I'm among the unsaved."

"And how long have you served as the pastor at St. Veronica's Parish?" Geraldine asks.

"Eight years," the witness says. "I was stationed in New Bedford before that, at the Church of St. Peter the Apostle."

"Thank you, Your Eminence." Geraldine glows again, as if her witness just provided us all with vital information. "Now, in the course of your service at St. Veronica's, did you come to know the Reverend Francis Patrick McMahon?"

"I did," he answers.

"Tell us about your getting to know each other, if you will, Your Eminence."

Harry turns to me and rolls his eyes farther back in his head than I'd have thought possible. I can't blame him; Geraldine's laying it on pretty thick. "I'm going to object like hell," he says, "as soon as she kisses his ring."

"Frank—Father McMahon—was already stationed at St. Veronica's when I was named pastor," Monsignor Davis says. "He'd been there five years at that point, stayed on another seven, until his death a year ago." The Monsignor shifts in the witness box and looks toward our table the first time, his gaze settling on Derrick Holliston. The priest's dark brown eyes are heavily lashed and unusually wide. They convey not a shred of reproach, but Holliston twists in his chair and stares at the side wall anyway.

"How many priests serve St. Veronica's Parish?" Geraldine asks.

"Two," he says. "We have plenty of visiting priests who help out during the summer months, when our Sunday Mass schedule triples, but only two of us are stationed there year-round."

"So am I correct in presuming, Your Eminence, that you and Father McMahon got to know each other fairly well during the seven years you served together?"

"We did," he says, turning his attention back to the jury. "Frank and I came to be great friends."

"Tell us about him," she says.

Harry's on his feet, headed for the bench. "Your Honor," he says, "I hate to interrupt my Sister Counsel."

His Sister Counsel knows better; there are few sports Harry enjoys more. She pivots and scowls at him.

"But I have to ask the court to set some parameters here," he says.

Judge Gould nods. Every lawyer in the room knows Harry's right—even Geraldine. Technically, this witness shouldn't be on the stand more than five minutes; he has precious little to say that's relevant. Since we've put the self-defense claim into play, he's entitled to opine that Father McMahon wasn't a violent man, that he had no propensity toward assault, sexual or otherwise. Beyond that, the dead priest's character is of no import. Murder is murder, whether the deceased was a nice guy or not.

Geraldine isn't happy with Harry's request, though, and she doesn't give a damn that he's right. Technical considerations notwithstanding, she'd like to keep the priest in the witness box all day. If the jurors like him, if they conclude he's a decent, moral man, they're likely to presume the same of his late colleague.

"Counselor," the judge says to her, "narrow your question, please."

She will, but not before she throws her hands in the air and shakes her blond head at the jurors. She's hamstrung, she's telling them. These two less-than-reasonable men are preventing her from telling the story as it should be told.

Harry backs up to our table, watching her performance, and remains standing in front of his chair. No point in sitting down again until he hears the new question.

Geraldine turns and smiles at him. "Where is Father McMahon buried?" she asks, still looking at Harry. He drops into his seat and sighs. The question is narrow, after all. It's also irrelevant, but an objection would be pointless.

"Behind the church," the witness answers. "There's a small cemetery back there, a dozen or so ancient graves clustered around a statue of Saint Veronica. Frank used to go out there in all sorts of weather to say his Divine Office."

Geraldine's eyebrows arch before she turns back to her witness. "Divine Office, Your Eminence?"

Harry stirs beside me but he doesn't stand. Again, the question is irrelevant but harmless. Harry Madigan is good at choosing his courtroom battles; Catholicism questions are fights he can forfeit.

"Canonical prayers," Monsignor Davis explains to the jurors, "prayers we priests recite every day. Frank liked to say his out behind the church. He seemed to find peace there, amid the centuries-old graves and the image of our parish's patron."

"Ah, Saint Veronica." Geraldine's somber expression suggests the witness just raised a critical point. "Tell us about her."

Judge Gould looks toward Harry, no doubt wondering how long he plans to let this line of questioning continue. When their eyes meet, they both cover their mouths quickly, using fake coughs to camouflage unexpected laughs. Between the two of them, they've handled every thug in the county, but neither has the chutzpah to bounce a lady saint from the courtroom. I lean into Harry and cluck like a chicken. Still he keeps his laughter in check, but his face turns beet-red from the effort.

"Veronica Giuliani," the Monsignor says, "a remarkable woman. She was born in Mercatello, a small village in Italy, in 1660. At seventeen, she joined the convent—the Poor Clares—against her wealthy father's wishes, I might add. Two decades later she received the stigmata."

"The stigmata?" Geraldine sounds like she just can't wait to find out what that's all about.

"Think our District Attorney is planning to convert?" Harry whispers.

"Only if they let her be the Pope," I tell him.

"Yes," the Monsignor says, "an amazing phenomenon. Historically, certain saints and blessed persons became known as stigmatics. They developed wounds—physical markings—that mirrored those inflicted upon Jesus Christ at the crucifixion. Veronica's stigmata met with a great deal of skepticism at first, as most of them did. But the Church conducted an extensive investigation and, after years of inquiry, determined there was every reason to believe her wounds were the result of divine action. Theologians have documented three hundred and twenty-one such cases since the thirteenth century. The first was Francis of Assisi."

Judge Gould looks like he's about ready to put a stop to all this, but Harry speaks up first. "Hey, Francis of Assisi," he says, as if the witness just mentioned a mutual childhood friend. "He's the animal guy."

The jurors all chuckle and Monsignor Davis does too. "That's right," he says, smiling at Harry. "Saint Francis is well known as the patron saint of animals."

Geraldine looks perturbed. No prosecutor wants levity injected into a murder trial, not even a few seconds of it. She's hard-pressed to complain, though. She led us down this path, after all.

"Ms. Schilling," the judge says, "I think we've gone pretty far afield here. Let's get back to the matter at hand, shall we?"

"Certainly, Your Honor." She sounds unusually agreeable, relieved even. Exploring the vagaries of Catholicism was fun until Harry piped up. "Your Eminence," she says, "tell us what you remember about last Christmas Eve."

Harry tenses beside me. Geraldine's not in foul territory yet, but she's batting in that direction.

"Well," the Monsignor says, "Frank and I always took turns celebrating the Christmas Vigil Mass. Last year was his turn." The priest pauses, looks out at the gallery, and shakes his head; for the first time since he took the stand, he looks sad, forlorn even. "Sometimes I wish it had been mine."

Geraldine waits while her witness pours a glass of water and sips.

"In any event," he says, "whichever one of us wasn't celebrating the Vigil always came over to help out with Communion. We normally have quite a large turnout on Christmas Eve. I helped Frank last year, and then went back across the street, to the rectory." He shakes his head again, his eyes lowered to his lap this time. "Not a day goes by that I don't regret it. Things might have turned out differently if I'd stayed."

He's right, of course. Things almost certainly would have turned out differently if he'd stayed. If Holliston's telling the truth, the presence of a third party would have nixed any amorous advances, real or imagined. If Holliston's lying, the two-to-one ratio might have scared him off, forced him to stalk an alternate quarry. But if Holliston had his heart set on going home with the Christmas Eve collection no matter what, St. Veronica's Parish probably would have ended up with two dead priests.

"But you went back to the chapel again later, is that right?" Geraldine turns away from the witness and walks slowly toward us, staring at Holliston and silently inviting the jurors to do likewise.

"I did," Monsignor Davis says. "Mass had started at seven. We'd finished with Holy Communion just before eight. Frank would've given the final blessing a few minutes after that. When he wasn't back at the rectory by nine, I went across the street to see what was keeping him."

"Were you worried?" Geraldine asks.

The Monsignor shakes his head. "Not at all," he says. "I fully expected to find Frank relaxed in one of the back pews, chewing the fat with a parishioner. That was his way; he always had time for a heart-to-heart or a good yarn."

"So what made you check on him?"

The Monsignor shrugs. "I figured I'd join them," he says, "Frank and whatever parishioner was enjoying a Christmas Eve visit with him."

Geraldine pauses, clasps her hands behind her back, and takes a deep breath. "Tell us, Your Eminence, what you found when you returned to the chapel that night."

Harry's up. "Absolutely not," he says.

Judge Gould nods; he knows what Harry's about to say. And he agrees. Geraldine has a half dozen graphic crime scene photographs in evidence. She doesn't get a verbal description as well.

"It's cumulative," Harry continues. "It's out of the question."

Monsignor Davis looks surprised. This is the first time he's heard Harry raise his voice.

"That's nonsense," Geraldine counters. "The Monsignor's entitled to tell us what he found when he went back to the church."

"No, he's not." Harry's directly in front of the judge, pointing back at Geraldine. "Not after she introduced multiple photographs of the scene. At this point, the prejudicial impact of this testimony far outweighs its probative value. It has no probative value. It's nothing but repetitive."

Judge Gould continues to nod. "Sustained," he says. "Monsignor Davis, please disregard the District Attorney's last question."

"Whatever you say," the witness answers.

"Ms. Schilling," the judge adds, "move on."

She gives another short performance for the jury—another thrust of her arms and shake of her head—and then plasters a resigned expression on her face. The judge has left her with no alternative; she'll have to get to the proper questions now. "Your Eminence," she says, "are you aware that the defendant in this case has raised a self-defense claim?"

"I am," he says. "I'm aware of that through your office." The Monsignor delivers his answer to Geraldine, but she's not looking at him. She's continuing her slow journey toward us, staring at Derrick Holliston's profile.

"You're aware, are you not, Your Eminence, that the defendant claims Father Francis Patrick McMahon made inappropriate sexual contact with him, that Father Francis Patrick McMahon became violent when his advances were rejected, so violent, in fact, that this defendant had no choice but to fight for his own life?"

The Monsignor is quiet for a moment, apparently unsure who he should speak to now that Geraldine is on the other side of the room. "I am," he says to the jurors. "I'm aware of those claims, all of them."

Geraldine stops smack in front of Holliston and turns to face the witness again. All outward appearances suggest she's completely calm, relaxed even, but I know better. She's on an adrenaline high. She doesn't say a word until the room falls silent. "Now I ask you, Your Eminence," she says quietly, "based upon your knowledge of Father Francis Patrick McMahon, based upon your knowledge of his character, based upon your observations of his conduct with third parties, based upon the totality of your experience with him, are this defendant's claims credible?"

Geraldine didn't point at Derrick Holliston until she said the last phrase, an extraordinary exercise of willpower on her part.

Monsignor Davis doesn't answer right away. He looks at the jurors, one at a time, as he seems to search for words. "They're not," he says at last. "They're simply not."

Geraldine doesn't move. Her index finger is still in Derrick Holliston's face, and she keeps it there while the Monsignor's words resonate through the silent courtroom. Finally, she drops her hand to her side and looks at Harry. "Your witness," she says.

Harry stands and smooths his suit coat, then walks toward the witness box, pointing a pen at its occupant. "No disrespect intended here," he says, "but I'm going to have trouble with this 'Your Emperor' thing."

"Your Honor!" Geraldine's on her feet, but Harry keeps going.

"Any reason I can't just call you Monsignor?"

Most of the jurors laugh now. Even Judge Gould struggles to suppress a smile. Dominic Davis wears his openly. "None at all," he says. "Monsignor will do nicely."

Geraldine shakes her head and drops back into her chair.

"Now about Veronica Giuliani," Harry says, "is she related to Rudy?"

More laughter, from the gallery, from the jury box, even from the bench. Geraldine is beside herself. There's not a hell of a lot she can do about it, though. She's the one who dragged Veronica into this in the first place.

"Could be." Monsignor Davis seems intrigued by the idea. "If the mayor were to trace his family tree back far enough, he might just bump into her."

Harry laughs. "So maybe old Rudy's related to a saint?"

The Monsignor takes a moment to consider and then smiles. "God calls each and every one of us to be a saint," he says.

Harry scratches his head. "I must've been out," he says. "And the big guy didn't leave a message."

"Your Honor, *please*." Geraldine's on her feet. "This is far beyond the scope of direct. My Brother Counsel is out of line."

Harry turns to face her. He looks offended. "Not so," he says. "I didn't know Veronica's last name until you, Sister Counsel, brought it to my attention. I'm entitled to explore."

Judge Gould leans forward on the bench and peers down at both of them over the tops of his dark-framed glasses. He looks like a frustrated parent dealing with perpetually bickering children. Gives a whole new meaning to the "Brother/Sister Counsel" phenomenon. "Mr. Madigan," he says, "I'm afraid your theological pursuits, admirable though they may be, will have to wait until another day, sir. Move on."

Harry feigns abject disappointment before turning back to the witness. "Monsignor Davis," he says, "the collection money disappeared last Christmas Eve, didn't it?"

"It did."

"Any estimate on how much money vanished?"

The Monsignor shrugs. "Our parishioners are quite generous all year round," he says, "but never more so than at Christmas and

Easter. Most years the Vigil collection brings in more than a thousand dollars."

"That's a lot of money," Harry says, "to have erased from your operating budget without warning."

"It is," the priest agrees.

"Anything else disappear that night?"

Monsignor Davis nods. "The monstrance," he says. "The holy monstrance was taken from the altar, the consecrated host within it."

"Yesterday afternoon, Monsignor, we heard testimony from Chatham's Chief Fitzpatrick."

The witness nods again.

"He told us you discovered Father McMahon's body in the sacristy last Christmas Eve, called the police, and *then* noticed the empty collection basket. Do you agree with that sequence of events?"

"I do," the priest says. "That's exactly how it happened."

"When did you notice the monstrance was missing?"

The question is perfectly proper, but Geraldine gets to her feet anyway. She does this frequently. It's her "I don't have an objection yet but give me a minute and I'll sure as hell come up with one" stance.

"Right away," Monsignor Davis says. "As soon as I entered the church, I saw that the altar was empty. I thought maybe Frank had taken the monstrance to the sacristy to polish it up a bit. Sometimes it gets smudged when we handle it, when we transfer it from its usual home in the Holy Tabernacle."

"When you called the police, did you mention the monstrance?"

"No." The Monsignor shakes his head. "I don't remember

what I said, to tell you the truth, but I'm certain I spoke of nothing but Frank."

"When did you mention it?"

"That night. I met with the Chief and another officer after the Medical Examiner's people took Frank's body away. I tried to explain the significance of the consecrated host, the urgency with which our parishioners would want it recovered, if possible."

"Did you meet with the Chief or other Chatham officers after that night?"

"Oh yes," the witness answers. "Several times."

"Give us a guesstimate," Harry says.

Monsignor Davis shrugs. "I don't know. Three, four times, maybe."

"What about our District Attorney?" Harry turns and smiles at her as he asks. She doesn't smile back. "How many times would you say you've met with her?"

"Five or six," the Monsignor says. "Again, though, I'm guessing."

"Did you mention the monstrance at each of those meetings?"

"I'm sure I did," the priest says. "It's been a constant concern."

"Would it be fair to say, Monsignor Davis, that during your multiple meetings with the Chatham police, and during your multiple meetings with our District Attorney, you expressed more urgency over the disappearance of the monstrance than you did over the missing money, the missing thousand-plus dollars?"

"Just a minute." Geraldine leaves her table and heads for the bench. It took a few moments, but she's come up with a beef. "This witness isn't a forensic expert," she says to the judge. "His 'sense of urgency' about a particular piece of evidence doesn't amount to a hill of beans."

Geraldine Schilling doesn't often make tactical mistakes, but

I'm pretty sure she's making one now. Trying to silence one's own witness is almost never a good idea. Harry actually laughs. "I missed the hill-of-beans class in law school," he says, "but I do believe my Sister Counsel is telling us this witness's opinion on the matter is irrelevant."

Judge Gould looks as if he's prepared to rule, but Harry keeps talking.

"That would be the same Sister Counsel who spent the last half hour discussing rectory staffing, canonical prayers, and stigmata," he says. "And now she raises a relevance objection to a question about a piece of evidence that was taken from the scene of the crime?"

"All right, Mr. Madigan," the judge says, his voice low. "That's enough."

Harry's not finished, though. He turns to the jurors. "That would be the same Sister Counsel who withheld the fact of that theft from the defense for an entire year." He points back toward our table. "Maybe our District Attorney would like to object to this man's having a trial at all. Maybe we're taking up too much of her time. Maybe it would be more convenient for her if we just lock him up now, ask questions later."

"Mr. Madigan!" Judge Gould bangs his gavel once, hard, to shut Harry up. "You've made your point," he says. "You may proceed." He sets his gavel down and turns to Geraldine. "Ms. Schilling, your objection is overruled."

She storms back to her table and Derrick Holliston jabs my arm with his elbow. He actually looks pleased when I turn to face him—a first. He narrows his eyes to slits and points his pen at Harry. "Now we're gettin' somewhere," he says.

I'm weary of him.

"Monsignor Davis," Harry continues, his voice raised as if he's still arguing, "can you answer the question, sir?"

The Monsignor looks flustered, his brown eyes even wider than usual. "What was it?" he asks.

Most of the jurors chuckle.

"Damned if I know," Harry says.

The entire panel laughs now. Geraldine is furious.

Harry points to the court reporter, an attractive, thirty-something brunette who's new to her courthouse job. She stops tapping at once and reaches for the narrow strip of encoded paper that snakes from the front of her machine. She searches for a few moments and then clears her throat. "'Would it be fair to say, Monsignor Davis,'" she recites in a monotone, "'that during your multiple meetings with the Chatham police, and during your multiple meetings with our District Attorney, you expressed more urgency over the disappearance of the monstrance than you did over the missing money, the missing thousand-plus dollars?'"

The Monsignor nods emphatically. "Absolutely," he says. "We hated to lose so much money, especially at that time of year. We try to help our less fortunate families make ends meet through the winter, when heating expenses are so steep, so the loss of the money was a real blow. But the theft of the monstrance—the theft of the Blessed Sacrament—was far worse."

"Tell us why," Harry says.

Generally speaking, lawyers ask questions that call for yes-or-no answers during cross-examinations. Even a witness who wants to elaborate on a particular point is normally barred from doing so during cross, forced to wait until redirect, if there is one. Not this witness, though. Harry will let Dominic Davis talk all day, as long as he's emphasizing the importance of the missing monstrance.

The Monsignor pauses now, seems to want to choose his words carefully. "The consecrated host," he says at last, "is the body of Our Lord Jesus Christ."

Maria Marzetti bows her head at the mention of the Lord's name. Cora Rowlands makes the sign of the cross; when she raises her hand to her forehead, I realize she's cradling rosary beads. Holliston notices too; he snorts and turns to stare at the side wall again.

"You must understand," the witness says, leaning toward the jury. He seems concerned that he hasn't made himself clear. "The consecrated host is not a *symbol* of Christ's body, it *is* his body."

Maria and Cora nod in agreement. The others don't react.

"We'll take your word on that," Harry says. "But what about the other two?"

"Other two?"

"Aren't there three of them?" Harry asks. "A trio?"

The Monsignor appears to be at a loss for a moment, but then he breaks into a smile. "You're referring to the Trinity," he says to Harry. "The Holy Trinity."

"Bingo," Harry says.

Geraldine jumps to her feet. She sees more levity coming and she wants to head it off at the pass. "We'll stipulate," she says, holding both hands up like a traffic cop. "For God's sake, let's not go down that path. We'll stipulate to the doctrine of the Trinity. Father, Son, and Holy Ghost."

"'They caught the last train for the coast,'" Harry half sings. Gregory Harmon laughs out loud, then covers his mouth and fires a facial apology to the judge.

"*Spirit,*" Monsignor Davis says to our District Attorney. "Since the Second Vatican Council, we call the third member of the Trinity the Holy Spirit."

Harry turns and gives Geraldine yet another smile, this one accompanied by a wink. "Been a while, heh, Counselor?"

"Mr. Madigan!" Judge Gould bangs his gavel again, kneading his temple with his free hand. Harry had better curb his editorial comments; the judge's patience is wearing thin. His little ditty was well worth it, though. The jurors are still laughing. And Geraldine Schilling is livid.

Harry nods up at the judge, then turns back to the witness. "The man in charge wants me to wrap it up here," he says to Monsignor Davis. "So let's talk turkey."

The Monsignor laughs a little. "Okay," he says. "Let's."

"Father McMahon was already dead when you entered the church last Christmas Eve, wasn't he?"

"Yes," the priest says, "he was."

"And you didn't see what happened to him, did you?"

Monsignor Davis hesitates.

"You saw the aftermath of what happened," Harry adds quickly, "but you didn't see the altercation itself—or any portion of it—or anything that led up to it."

This clarification seems to assuage the witness's concerns. "That's correct," he says. "I didn't."

"And it's equally true to say you didn't hear any portion of it, isn't it, Monsignor?"

"Yes, that's equally true."

"So what you've offered us here today, Monsignor Davis, is your opinion, isn't it? You've testified to your *opinion* about what Father McMahon may or may not have done that night."

Again the priest hesitates and again Harry jumps in quickly to clarify. "In other words, Monsignor, your testimony isn't based on anything you perceived through your physical senses, is that correct?"

Still, the witness seems reluctant. "That is correct," he says after a moment. "But bear in mind that my vocation—my life's work—isn't based on anything I perceive through my earthly senses, either."

Harry should have seen that answer coming, but he didn't. It's written on his face. And there's no way in hell he wants to end the cross-examination on that note. "In any case," he says, pretending the prior response is of no significance, "you're not here today under subpoena, are you?"

"No, I'm not."

"You're here voluntarily, having told the District Attorney there was no need for a subpoena, is that correct?"

"Yes. That's correct."

"And Monsignor, your voluntary appearance here today is explainable—at least in part—by the fact that Francis Patrick McMahon was your good friend, isn't that true?"

"In part," the witness says. "Yes, I agree with that."

"Is it fair to say you felt you owed Father McMahon that much? Is it fair to say that by showing up here today voluntarily you hoped to honor your good friend's memory, to seek some semblance of justice for his untimely death?"

Monsignor Davis is quiet. He seems to have aged on the witness stand; his demeanor is subdued, his complexion pale. "I suppose that is true," he says at last. "Certainly the part about honoring Frank's memory." He pauses and tilts his head to one side. "But perhaps a man can't do that answering lawyer questions."

Now it's Harry's turn to be quiet. "Perhaps not," he says after a moment. He turns away from the witness, walks toward our table, but then stops. "About the weapon," he says, turning back to face the witness. "Where did it come from?"

Harry's only asking this question because he already knows the answer. He wouldn't dare otherwise.

"It was in the sacristy," the priest says. "The chapel is an old building; we're constantly making minor repairs, it seems. We keep a wooden box—a crate, I guess you'd call it—on one side of the counter. It's full of hammers, pliers, screwdrivers—all sorts of tools. The ice pick was among them."

"Thank you. And one last thing, Monsignor." Harry's still standing in the middle of the room, still facing the witness. "I want to offer you my sincere condolences on the loss of your good friend."

Some defense lawyers routinely offer condolences at the beginnings of cross-examinations, hoping at least some prosecution witnesses will let down their guards, perceive the defender as an ally of sorts. Harry doesn't. He's offered his sympathy to this witness—at the end of cross—because he means it.

Monsignor Davis seems to sense as much. He swallows a lump in his throat, then takes another sip of water. "I go out there—to the small cemetery—to pray for Frank every morning," he says to Harry. "And when I finish, I pray for Mr. Holliston."

Harry's surprise is genuine. We don't often meet a prosecution witness who prays for the accused. He looks from Monsignor Davis to Holliston, and then back to the priest again. "Thanks," he says as he sits.

The Monsignor nods.

Holliston leans forward, not looking the least bit pleased anymore. His face is scrunched into a maze of hatred and disbelief.

"Thanks?" he says too loudly. "*Thanks?*" He points at the witness box. "That guy calls me a liar and you say *thanks?* For Chrissake, whose side are you on?"

Harry stares back at our client, but says nothing. And there's a reason for that, of course. He doesn't know whose side he's on.

CHAPTER 22

Criminal defense lawyers lose. It's what we do. We lose when we know we should. We lose when we think we shouldn't. And we lose when we're damned certain we should carry the day. It's the nature of the beast.

It's odd, then, to watch Harry worry about winning. He's been tense in his chair beside me throughout our fifteen-minute break, his hands clutching the armrests, his eyes closed. He doesn't open them when the guards usher Derrick Holliston back to our table, but he does when Big Red comes through the side door with the jurors. Harry's quick to change his posture now, too, sitting up straighter, making eye contact with each member of the panel who'll allow it, adopting a serious, confident demeanor.

"Mr. Madigan," Judge Gould says when the last juror is seated, "you may proceed now, sir."

"Reasonable doubt," Harry says as he stands. "When all is said and done, this case boils down to one issue: reasonable doubt."

He unbuttons his suit coat and shoves his hands into his pockets as he leaves our table. "Judge Gould will instruct you that the Commonwealth bears the burden of proving every element of the crime charged beyond a reasonable doubt."

He stops in front of Geraldine's table and glances at her, then resumes his trip toward the jury box. "The judge will also tell you that proof beyond a reasonable doubt is proof that leaves you *firmly convinced* of the defendant's guilt."

Those are the exact words the judge will use in his instructions to the jury. Judges and lawyers routinely invoke the concept of reasonable doubt, but the truth is we've never been very good at defining it. Until fairly recently, the judge would have told the jurors that reasonable doubt exists if they "cannot say they feel an abiding conviction, to a moral certainty, of the truth of the charge." But a couple of years ago, the United States Supreme Court expressly disapproved of that language, noting that the term *moral certainty* has an entirely different meaning today than it did when the words were first penned by the Massachusetts Supreme Court in 1850.

"Firmly convinced," Harry repeats. "You should convict Mr. Holliston of murder only if you are *firmly convinced* that he did *not* act in self-defense."

Harry turns and looks at Geraldine again. "And you can't be," he adds. "Not on the evidence produced in this courtroom."

Geraldine stares back at him, seemingly unfazed by his focus on her. She's known Harry Madigan a long time, though; she knows he's just warming up.

Harry shifts his attention from Geraldine to our table before facing the jury again. "There are a few things we know for sure," he continues. He spreads his arms wide and leans on the railing of the jury box. "We know Mr. Holliston admitted his role in Father McMahon's death from the outset. We know he told the Chief of Police about the unwelcome sexual advances, and about the ensuing struggle, on the morning of his arrest. And we know he stuck to his guns during every subsequent interview; he never wavered."

A few of the jurors have pens in their hands, notepads on their laps. No one's writing anything, though. They're motionless. Harry has their undivided attention.

"And that's not all we know," he says, his voice growing louder. Geraldine stiffens even before he wheels around. "We know the District Attorney's office concealed evidence." His voice is booming now. "Critical evidence."

Geraldine looks up and meets Harry's accusing eyes. Clarence doesn't.

"Why did they do that?" Harry turns back to the jurors, inviting the fourteen of them to speculate on the prosecutors' motivations. "Why did they conceal a material fact from the defense?"

The spectators stir and Harry waits, as if he thinks someone else in the room might answer his question. He doesn't. He's waiting for quiet. "I'll give you one reason," he says when the silence is complete. "They did it because the missing monstrance blows yet another hole in this sorry excuse for a case, another hole in a case that already looks like Swiss cheese."

He walks slowly across the room and points at Geraldine, no doubt a first for both of them. "Our District Attorney would have you believe Mr. Holliston entered St. Veronica's Chapel last Christmas Eve intending to commit a felony. She'd have you believe he killed Father McMahon in the course of committing that felony."

Harry stops pointing, but he stays planted smack in front of Geraldine. "But there's a problem with our District Attorney's theory," he says quietly. "She has no evidence to support it."

Geraldine exhales as Harry leaves her table and walks toward ours. "Not one shred of evidence ties this man to *anything* that was taken from the chapel that night. And who knows what else is missing?"

"Your *Honor*!" Geraldine's on her feet, incensed by Harry's not-so-veiled suggestion that she may be hiding even more.

Judge Gould doesn't look sympathetic. "This is argument, Counsel," is all he says. Geraldine looks indignant as she drops back into her chair.

"Now," Harry continues as if neither Geraldine nor the judge said a word, "let's talk about the evidence we *do* have." He points at the empty witness box. "The Commonwealth called three men to this stand, credible individuals one and all. And every one of them gave you crucial information—critical facts—that support Mr. Holliston's version of the events that transpired last Christmas Eve."

Harry pauses in front of our table, picks up a pen and points it at the panel. "Think about that," he says. "The prosecution's witnesses—every one of them—buttressed Mr. Holliston's case."

It's clear from the jurors' expressions that they are thinking about it. They're not necessarily on the same page with Harry, though. More than a few brows knit. They want him to elaborate.

"First we heard from Calvin Ramsey," he says, "our Medical Examiner. And though our District Attorney questioned him for more than an hour and a half, she failed to elicit one fact during his direct examination that contradicted what Mr. Holliston has told law enforcement from the beginning. Not one."

Harry begins a slow stroll back toward the panel. "Dr. Ramsey delivered a critical fact during cross, though. He told you the medical evidence supports only one conclusion: Mr. Holliston and the deceased were face-to-face throughout the altercation. Medical evidence doesn't lie, ladies and gentlemen. And face-to-face combat isn't consistent with a robbery—certainly not a planned robbery—no matter how you slice it."

He pauses and fills a paper cup with water at the vacant witness stand. A few jurors jot notes as he drinks. "Next we heard from Chief Thomas Fitzpatrick," he says, crumpling the cup and tossing it into the plastic trash can near Dottie Bearse's desk, "a stand-up guy if ever there was one. Such a stand-up guy, in fact, that he outed our District Attorney."

"Your *Honor*!" Geraldine Schilling has probably never heard herself described as outed before.

Judge Gould shakes his head at her, says nothing. Nondisclosure doesn't go over well in his courtroom, intentional or not. On this issue, he's giving Harry free rein.

Harry stands still, looking up at the bench, letting the jurors absorb the judge's non-verbal response to our District Attorney's protest. "And finally," he says, turning back to the panel, "this morning we heard from Monsignor Davis. We heard about all sorts of things during his direct examination, didn't we? None of it had a damned thing to do with this case, but it was interesting, nonetheless."

More than a few jurors seem to agree with him; they nod and look from him to Geraldine, then back again. He leans on the jury box railing. "The Monsignor did have two things to tell us that matter, but our District Attorney didn't raise either one. Only during cross-examination did the witness get to address two issues that actually bear on this case. They're important. Keep them in mind."

A couple of the note-takers shift in their seats, pens poised.

"First," Harry says, "let's talk about the weapon, the ice pick. Monsignor Davis told you it belongs to the parish. It was in a wooden crate, a toolbox of sorts, on the sacristy counter. It's *not* something Derrick Holliston brought with him that night. So our District Attorney would have you believe Mr. Holliston went to St. Veronica's Chapel intending to rob the collection money, prepared to kill anyone who tried to stop him, but he didn't bother to bring a weapon along. He simply assumed there'd be one on hand."

Harry stands up straight and turns to look at Geraldine again. "Or maybe she'd have you believe he did bring a weapon, but then decided to look around the room and shop for a different one once he got there."

Harry faces the panel, his hands in his pants pockets again. "Common sense, ladies and gentlemen," he says. "The District Attorney's theories don't hold water."

He starts walking back toward the prosecutors' table and I'm pretty sure everyone in the courtroom knows what's coming. Geraldine does, anyway. She folds her arms across her chest and squares her shoulders. "Now," Harry says quietly, staring at her, "let's talk about the monstrance."

He doesn't, though. He doesn't talk about anything for what seems like a full minute. He finishes his trip to the prosecutors' table and stands facing them, his profile to the jury. Clarence fidgets, fussing with files, documents, and legal pads. Geraldine doesn't. She sits perfectly still, staring back at Harry, seemingly more than prepared to deflect whatever hand grenade he's about to lob at her.

"Monsignor Davis told us he met with Chatham police officers three or four times," Harry says at last. "And he met with our District Attorney five or six times. And at every meeting—*every* meeting—he brought up the topic of the missing monstrance, stressed its significance to him and his parish."

Harry leans toward Geraldine, his arms spread wide, palms down on her table. She stares at his tie. "Yet our District Attorney chose *not* to mention that significant topic to us," he says, his voice barely more than a whisper.

No one else in the courtroom makes a sound. Harry waits patiently until the silence is physically uncomfortable; even Geraldine, stoic until now, succumbs to a hard swallow. "Our District Attorney charged Mr. Holliston with first-degree murder," he says at last, pointing at Geraldine again, "a charge that carries a mandatory life sentence, a sentence to be served in the Walpole Penitentiary, a sentence that won't end until after he draws his last breath. And for a solid year after she issued that charge, she hid a critical fact—an *exculpatory* critical fact—from the accused and his attorneys."

Another hefty silence. Even Clarence is still, his fidgeting abandoned for the moment, his eyes lowered to the table.

"Bear in mind," Harry says as he stands up straight and faces the jurors again, "our District Attorney didn't rectify the situation voluntarily. She got *caught*."

All fourteen jurors look at Geraldine now. She doesn't look back at them, doesn't react to Harry's words at all.

"This is Derrick John Holliston's trial," Harry says as he walks toward our table, "no one else's. But the system governing this trial belongs to all of us; don't lose sight of that. *We* are responsible for our system. *We* are accountable for its integrity." Harry turns and fires yet another pointed stare at Geraldine. "*We* are blameworthy for its lack thereof."

She sighs and shakes her head at him, but she doesn't speak. An objection would be pointless; Judge Gould has made that perfectly clear.

"And don't forget," Harry says, "we're not only responsible for this system of ours; we're subject to it as well. Its integrity should be of grave concern to every last one of us."

He turns back to the panel. "You saw the crime-scene photographs, ladies and gentlemen. You don't need me to tell you that *wasn't* the scene of a robbery. It was the scene of a sexual assault. It was the scene of panic, of outrage."

With that, Harry walks behind our table and drops into his chair. The courtroom is soundless. Not one juror moves a muscle.

Even Holliston seems almost pleased with Harry's closing argument. "About time," he says as soon as Harry reclaims his seat. "It's about time you told it like it is."

Harry doesn't even look at him. He leans on his elbows, hands clasped, and stares straight ahead.

"You did a good job," I whisper. "They listened. You were effective."

He takes his glasses off and throws them on top of a legal pad before he looks at me. "That's great," he says, shielding his mouth from the jury with his hand. "Wrong. But effective."

CHAPTER 23

"Outrage," Geraldine says as she stands. "I find it surprising, baffling even, that the defense would speak of outrage."

She sorts through the stack of glossies on her table, the exhibits introduced during Tommy Fitzpatrick's testimony, and selects one. Everybody in the courtroom knows which one she's chosen. She covers the distance to the jury box slowly, in silence, then holds the photograph up in front of the panel. "We, as a civilized society, are the ones who should be outraged."

The jurors split evenly. Half revisit the scene of the dead priest sprawled on the slate floor of the sacristy, his blood-soaked cassock twisted, his shattered glasses nearby. Half don't. Cora Rowlands squeezes her eyes shut tight, the set of her jaw telling us she doesn't even want to be in the same *room* with that photo any longer. Gregory Harmon glances over at her and then pats her hand on their shared armrest; he looks concerned.

"That man," Geraldine continues, still displaying the glossy as she turns to point at our table, "did this. He admits it. But he wants you to excuse him; he wants you to say he's not responsible for what he did. Why? Because he wants you to buy into his cockamamie self-defense claim. He wants you to believe that this fifty-seven-year-old man attacked him, that the attack was so threatening, so brutal, he had no choice but to do *this* to protect himself."

She turns away from them abruptly and barrels toward us. Geraldine Schilling has raised steamrolling in spiked heels to a performance art. "This man," she says, pointing at Holliston, "wants you to believe he had to stab Father McMahon eight times to protect himself, eight times before he could get away from the middle-aged priest."

Geraldine raises a fist in the air and slams it downward, stopping just inches from Holliston's shoulder. He doesn't react. "One," she says. Again, she raises her fist and then thrusts it down at him. "Two."

She continues the count, in no hurry to finish, each imaginary stab more forceful than the last, each number called out a little louder. Holliston doesn't even flinch.

The blanket of silence that covers this courtroom is complete, pierced only by Geraldine's recitation, but she's shouting anyhow by the time she reaches *seven*. She stays planted in front of our table, turns away from Holliston, and delivers the final blow toward the jurors. "Eight," she bellows.

No one moves. Not a single juror. Not Holliston. Not Geraldine. Her fist remains suspended in midair. "How many puncture wounds did it take before Father McMahon staggered backward?" she says at last. "How many times did Derrick John Holliston stab Francis Patrick McMahon before the priest dropped to the floor?"

She lowers her still-clenched fist to her side, finally, and walks back toward the jury box. "Did Father McMahon reel after the second puncture? After the third? Did he fall after the fourth? The fifth?" She stops in front of the jury box and slaps her open palms on its railing. A few of the jurors jump. "Did it take *eight*?"

She turns and glares at Holliston, then faces the panel again. "I think not," she whispers. "That man," she says, pointing at us once more, "is a murderer. And like the vast majority of murderers, he's also a liar."

Calling the defendant a liar is a controversial topic among prosecutors. They all argue routinely that various defendants' claims are untrue, of course. But the use of the word *liar* is thought by some to be inappropriate, to demean the system. Not by Geraldine Schilling, though. She used to lecture me about it frequently when I worked for the District Attorney's office. "If you're going to ask a dozen people to go into the jury room and decide the defendant's a liar," she always said, "you damn well better have the guts to call him one in open court. But don't bother," she often added, "unless you can say it like you mean it."

Geraldine can. "A liar," she repeats. "His defense is a fabrication. It's a story he told no one until he was arrested for the priest's murder. It's a story he told no one until he was confronted with indisputable evidence of his own guilt. It's a story he told no one until he was caught, until he was trapped like a rat."

The jurors are attentive, focused. Their faces reveal nothing.

"An entire week elapsed between Father McMahon's murder and this defendant's arrest," Geraldine continues, "and he told no one of this brutal attack he claims to have suffered at the priest's hands."

She half laughs. "This defendant—this murderer, this liar—is trying to sell you a bill of goods, ladies and gentlemen. Don't let him. One man—and one man only—was attacked in St. Veronica's sacristy last Christmas Eve." She holds up the glossy again; she's had it in her hand throughout her argument. "This one."

Even fewer members of the panel choose to look at the grisly crime scene this time. Geraldine doesn't try to force the issue. She lowers the photo to her side after just a few seconds—a wise decision, I think. These jurors have about had it.

"Mr. Madigan spoke with you at great length about reasonable doubt," Geraldine says. "I don't plan to do so. On the subject of reasonable doubt, I tell you only one thing: the operative word is *reasonable*."

A few jurors nod at her. A few others jot quick reminders in their notepads.

"Mr. Madigan also spoke with you at length about the monstrance," she says, "about my failure to disclose its disappearance. Again, I don't plan to say much about it. On the matter of my failure to disclose the missing monstrance to the defense, I tell you two things. First, it was a mistake, my mistake. And second, it doesn't have anything to do with the defendant's guilt or innocence; it doesn't amount to a hill of beans."

Geraldine folds her arms, pressing the glossy to her side, its blank, white back facing outward. "The defendant would have you believe that a man with no history of violence, a Catholic priest who led a life of prayer, a life of service to others, suddenly— at the age of fifty-seven—revealed his never-before-seen diabolical side. And he did it on one of the holiest nights of the year."

She half laughs again. "That, ladies and gentlemen, is the theory of this case that doesn't hold water. Men who are violent tend to mellow in middle age," she says. "It doesn't work the other way around."

She paces the length of the jury box, her arms still folded, her head tilted toward the panel. "Common sense, ladies and gentlemen. This case isn't about unwanted sexual advances. It isn't about fending off forced attentions. And it certainly isn't about self-defense."

They stare at her, rapt, all fourteen of them. Still, their faces reveal nothing.

"We all know what happened here," she says as she comes to a stop near the middle of the box. She raises her favorite glossy again, says nothing.

Three-quarters of the jurors avert their eyes this time around; Cora Rowlands isn't the only one who's reached the saturation point. But Geraldine *does* intend to force the issue now. She waits, her silence suggesting she'll stand there for the rest of the month if that's what it takes to get them to view the bloody scene one last time. And one by one, they do. All but Cora.

"This is what happened," our District Attorney says at last. "A holy place. A holy man. An unholy crime."

Chapter 24

"Relax," Harry says as he drops into the chair across from mine. "It's Friday. Maybe he went out for a beer."

I stare across the table at him, drumming my fingers on the red Formica. "When was the last time you saw him go out for a beer at two in the afternoon?"

The Kydd isn't answering the phones again. And we've already learned what that means: nothing good.

"Well, then maybe he's doing a little Christmas shopping. 'Tis the season, you know." Harry leans closer and lowers his voice. "Tell the truth," he says. "What do you think he'll get for me?"

I frown. Even he doesn't believe the Kydd is shopping. We're back at the Piccadilly, where today's special is a fried clam roll, with fries and slaw on the side. Harry ordered two. He needs to keep his strength up, he said, while the jury deliberates. He also ordered a cranberry muffin for me—grilled and buttered—and I've all but finished it. Trial is over, after all. There's nothing to do now but wait.

"I just wish he'd return my messages, tell us what the hell is going on."

"Don't worry," Harry says, squeezing open the spout of his second chocolate milk. "We've only been out of the courthouse twenty minutes. And besides, bad news keeps, remember?"

He's right. That's precisely why I'm on edge.

"Oh, look," he says, sounding delighted, "it's the God Squad." He waves toward the door, as if he's hailing a cab, so I turn to find out who's here. It's Geraldine, with Monsignor Davis in tow.

The Piccadilly doesn't often host a monsignor, of course, but it's even more surprising to see Geraldine Schilling in here. The deli doesn't allow smoking. And everyone in the Barnstable County Complex knows our District Attorney doesn't eat, ever. Caffeine and nicotine sustain her.

"Over here," Harry calls, still waving at them. "Join us, Your Émigré. And by all means, bring your friend."

Oddly enough, he does. They cross the room and stand beside our table, coats buttoned up tight. The Monsignor smiles at us. Geraldine doesn't. "What a surprise," she says to Harry, running her leather gloves across her palm as she takes in the twin platters. "You're snacking."

He grins up at both of them and points to his second meal, as yet untouched. "Help yourselves," he says. "There's plenty more where that came from."

Geraldine scowls; she'd sooner swallow arsenic. The Monsignor laughs and takes a few fries.

"What keeps you in our midst, Padre?" Harry sticks a thumb out at Geraldine. "You're not trying to save her wretched soul, are you?"

Monsignor Davis laughs again, then grows serious. "The Kendricks are part-time parishioners," he says. "I thought I might be of some assistance to them, offer some spiritual support."

Harry sets his half-eaten clam roll on the cardboard platter.

My stomach knots. "The Kendricks? What about them? Why do they need support, spiritual or otherwise?"

The Monsignor looks suddenly worried. He doesn't answer; he turns to Geraldine instead, giving her the floor. She has news, apparently, and before she says a word, I know exactly what it is. "Charles Kendrick is in custody," she tells me, pointing toward the courthouse. "I thought you'd want to know. He's in lockup now; Chatham's finest ran him in at my direction. Your associate is with him."

So much for the Kydd's shopping spree.

"Arraignment is scheduled for five," she says. "I expect you'll want to hang around for it."

"Five? All the players are here now. What are we waiting for?" Not that I'm in any big hurry. Harry was right. Bad news keeps.

"To accommodate the family," she says. "They want to attend. And they can't get here before then."

I shake my head. "They're in Chatham. They could be here in forty minutes." I realize my mistake before I finish the sentence.

"Not that family," she says. "The Forresters. They asked that we give them enough time to make the drive from Stamford."

Of course they did. Warren, Catherine, and Meredith want to hear Geraldine's evidence against the Senator firsthand. They want to look him in the eye, if they can get close enough. They want to ask the question all murder victims' families ask, the one that burns in their hearts, the one that's never adequately answered. *Why?*

Geraldine turns and heads for the door, her mission apparently accomplished. Monsignor Davis starts to follow, but he pauses and rests a hand on my shoulder. "I'll say a prayer," he says.

"Thanks," I tell him. "I'd ask for a word or two of your Divine Office, but that's only for priests. And I'm not even a Catholic." I'd never heard of the Divine Office until he testified this morning, but I don't tell him that part.

He smiles again, and it's genuine. "Doesn't matter," he says, giving my shoulder a squeeze. "Prayer helps us all."

With that, he leaves, and for a split second I wish I *were* Catholic, a notion I've never stumbled upon before. It's a fleeting fancy, of course, but at the moment I'm not certain of anything. Faith might help. I wish mine weren't so riddled with doubt.

I also wish I hadn't eaten the damned muffin.

CHAPTER 25

We're in lockup. We've been here for the better part of three hours now: Charles Kendrick, the Kydd, and I. Our client's mantra hasn't wavered. "I don't have any idea," he tells us again and again. "I don't know anything about it. I swear."

"Our District Attorney has been wrong in the past," I tell him, "but she's never been sloppy. She had you hauled in here; that means she's got evidence. If you know what the evidence is—or even what it might be—it would behoove you to give us a heads-up. I'm tired of running this race a lap behind Geraldine Schilling."

"I don't," he says, looking from me to the Kydd, as if the Kydd might back him up. "I swear to God I don't know what evidence she could have. I would never lift a hand to Michelle. I had nothing to do with her death."

Maybe politicians are particularly persuasive by nature. Or maybe I'm going soft in my middle age. Whatever the reason, I believe him. Part of me wishes I didn't. *Someone* murdered Michelle Forrester. I hate to think of that someone still roaming the Cape.

A series of knocks quiets us and then the door opens. "It's time," a uniformed guard says as he and his partner crowd into the small room. Senator Kendrick's wrists are already cuffed behind his back, as they have been all afternoon, but the second guard through the door approaches him now with ankle shackles. "Is that necessary?" I ask.

The guard looks from me to the Senator, who's sitting quietly at a small table, his shoulders stooped, his eyes lowered to the floor. Not exactly the portrait of a combative prisoner; not the profile of a flight risk, either. The uniform consults silently with his partner and then shrugs. "I guess not," he says, dropping the heavy hardware on the table and beckoning his charge with one hand. "Let's go, Senator," he says, his tone neutral. "It's time."

Charles Kendrick and his escorts enter the main courtroom of the District Courthouse first, the Kydd and I bringing up the rear. The noise in the enormous room escalates as soon as the first trio clears the doorway, before I can even see inside. No doubt the crowd is reacting to the sight of our senior senator in cuffs. I'm startled by the volume, and one look at the Kydd tells me he is too. The place must be packed.

It is. The spectators assembled in Superior Court for the conclusion of the Holliston trial earlier today have moved here en masse, it seems, and they've got plenty of new companions. Half the year-round residents of North Chatham are here, Helene Wilson among them, about a half dozen rows back. Her gaze moves from the Senator to me and she shakes her head. Her eyes are worried.

Members of the press corps jockey for the front spots in the side aisles, forced by court officers to stay pressed against the windowless walls in single file. The officers are trying to keep some semblance of an aisle open on each side of the room, but I'm pretty sure a fire in this building now would kill us all.

Most of the reporters call out urgent questions—to Senator Kendrick, to the Kydd, to me—as we approach our table. We ignore them, but they continue shouting at us anyway. They're wired. The Senator's arrest isn't just a scoop; it's a scandal.

Honey Kendrick is already here, seated in the front row, directly behind our table. Abby sits on one side of her, holding her mother's hand. Monsignor Davis is on the other, seated sideways and talking quietly with both of them. Mother and daughter are in tears; the Monsignor is undoubtedly doing his best to console them. His job is going to get harder as we proceed. Geraldine Schilling has news to share, a story to tell. None of us wants to hear it, Honey and Abby least of all.

The counsel tables in District Court are normally surrounded by too many olive green, imitation leather, high-backed chairs. Today, when we could use a few, only two are pulled up to the defense table. The Kydd points to the empty seats at the bar, telling me he'll sit back there.

"Not on your life," I tell him. "You're not going anywhere, Kydd. Find another chair and sit right here. You've been on this case longer than I have today." *Misery loves company* is my real rationale. I'm pretty sure the Kydd knows that, but he retrieves another chair from against the side wall without argument. No sooner does he sit than the room falls abruptly silent. And silence—in this arena, anyhow—is the ultimate attention-getter.

The sudden quiet prompts those of us seated up front to shift in our chairs. Geraldine and Clarence turn to the gallery and the Kydd, the Senator, and I do likewise. The explanation stares back at us. The Forresters—Mom, Dad, and big sister—are just inside the back doors, looking straight ahead at our table, at the Senator, at the man they've been told murdered Michelle. Not one of us moves. Even at this distance, their expressions shut us down. They're stricken. In pain. And it's physical.

The chambers door opens and the bailiff tells us to rise. I'm surprised when the judge emerges—pleasantly so. All arraignments are held in District Court and most are presided over by District Court judges. The chief judge apparently made a special request on behalf of our senior senator, though. Leon Long is here for this one, and he ordinarily presides in Superior Court.

Judge Long is the only black judge ever to sit in Barnstable County. And no matter which bench he's on, he's a welcome sight to members of the defense bar. In his courtroom, the presumption of innocence is real and the prosecution's burden is steep. He bangs his gavel before he sits—a habit engrained over the course of more than two decades on the bench—but it's not necessary. The Forrester family has already called this room to order.

The courtroom clerk stands, recites the docket number, and then announces, "The Commonwealth of Massachusetts versus Charles Johnson Kendrick." She looks over at us—not unkindly—and then reclaims her seat.

Geraldine is up instantly. "Your Honor," she says, "Mr. Kendrick is charged with the first-degree murder of Michelle Andrea Forrester, a murder committed with extreme atrocity or cruelty."

Some prosecutors might address the Senator as *Mister* by mistake. Not Geraldine. From this moment until she secures his conviction and sentence, Geraldine Schilling will seize every opportunity she can to diminish Charles Kendrick. Stripping him of his title is just the beginning. It's nothing personal; she does it to all murder defendants. In her mind, at least, it's part of the job.

Judge Long looks at me and shakes his head, ever so slightly. The signal is almost imperceptible, but it's there. And I've tried enough cases before him to know what he's telling me. He doesn't want to hear the Senator's plea yet. He wants the District Attorney to put her cards on the table first. "Ms. Schilling," he says, "let's hear the facts."

Most Barnstable County judges will take a simple plea from the defendant—guilty or not—before they call for a recitation of the facts. Not Leon Long. In his courtroom, the defendant need not say a word until the government demonstrates it's got something real against him. Geraldine doesn't need to prove her case at this point, of course. But she does need to convince the judge she has one.

She seems ready to do just that. "As you are undoubtedly aware, Your Honor, Ms. Forrester went missing last Thursday, eight days ago. She was last seen at Cape Cod Community College, wrapping up a press conference for her employer." Geraldine stops and points at the Senator. "Counselor," Judge Long says, "there's no need to point. I'm well aware of the defendant's seat assignment."

Judge Long has given her this admonition before—many times in many cases. Pointing is part of the drama prosecutors put on for jurors; it has no place in an arraignment. Geraldine won't stop, though. She can't help herself. She looks up at the judge now, her expression suggesting he just paid her a hefty compliment. "The facts," he reminds her.

"Of course, Your Honor," she says. "Charles Kendrick was one of the first witnesses we interviewed. I spoke with him personally, Monday morning and again Monday afternoon. On both occasions, he claimed he had no contact with the deceased after the Four Cs press conference."

Geraldine looks over at us and almost smiles before she continues. "The deceased's automobile, a BMW roadster, was found on Tuesday, parked deep in the woods near the intersection of Old Queen Anne and Training Field roads in Chatham."

I turn to check in with the Kydd, then with the Senator. They're as surprised as I am. The area Geraldine is referring to is known as the Golden Triangle, eighteen acres of pristine wooded conservation land. This is the first any of us has heard of Michelle's car being found there.

"That's right," Geraldine says, speaking in our direction now. "We withheld that fact from the public, pending the results of forensic testing."

Geraldine returns to her table and Clarence hands her three documents, no doubt the results to which she just referred. She delivers one copy to us, passes another up to the judge, and holds on to the third. "Hair follicles and skin fragments," she says, tapping the top page. "Multiple samples. *All* match those of the deceased."

I pass our copy of the lab report to the Kydd so he can check her facts. I'm virtually certain she's calling it like it is, though. Geraldine Schilling usually does.

The judge studies his copy of the report, then peers over the rims of his half-glasses. "That's to be expected," he says to Geraldine. "It was her car."

"True," she says. "That *is* to be expected." She turns and walks slowly toward us, her eyes holding the Senator's. "But not in the trunk."

A single sob fills the room, then ends abruptly. Catherine Forrester sits in the front row behind the prosecutors' table, across the aisle from Monsignor Davis and the Kendricks, with both hands pressed over her mouth. Her eyes are squeezed shut and two rivers course down her cheeks. She's flanked by Warren and Meredith, both trying in vain to comfort her, both fighting losing battles with their own floodgates.

Geraldine waits, longer than necessary, still staring at the Senator. "Counselor," Judge Long says quietly, "continue."

"Blood," she says, looking up at him. "We also found a solitary—but sizable—patch of blood on the upholstery in the trunk. It, too, matches that of the deceased."

The judge nods and looks down at the lab report again. Geraldine goes back to her table, retrieves an evidence bag, and hands it up to him. "And this," she says. "A rope, approximately eighteen inches in length."

Judge Long scrutinizes the bag, then looks back at Geraldine. "Ordinary clothesline," he says.

"Exactly," she agrees as she pivots and walks toward us again. "What we *didn't* find," she says, "is the spare. The BMW roadster's spare tire is ordinarily stored in the trunk. Michelle Forrester's was missing." She slaps a hand on our table and the Senator jumps a little beside me. "Until this morning," she says, glaring at him.

Senator Kendrick stares back at her, then at me, and shakes his head. He doesn't know what she's talking about.

"As we all know," she says, turning away from him and facing the bench again, "Chatham's harbormaster found Ms. Forrester's body yesterday, floating in the shallows of Pleasant Bay."

Catherine breaks down again. Geraldine pauses, allowing the mother's sobs to take center stage. There's no other sound in the crowded courtroom.

"Our Medical Examiner performed the autopsy yesterday," she says at last. She retrieves another set of documents from Clarence and again delivers copies to us and to the judge. "This is his report."

I check the signature line, then pass it over to the Kydd. Calvin Ramsey had a long day yesterday.

"Cause of death," she says, holding up her copy of the autopsy report, "cerebral hemorrhage."

Catherine's sobs had softened, but they escalate again. Geraldine turns to look at her. "Induced by blunt trauma to the cranium," she says quietly, "a single heavy blow to the skull. The absence of water in the lungs indicates she was dead before her body was dumped into the ocean."

All three Forresters are audibly crying now. Everyone else in the room is silent. The Senator is rigid beside me; he doesn't seem to be breathing.

"My office secured a search warrant this morning," Geraldine continues as she marches toward us yet again, "for the Kendrick property on Old Harbor Road in North Chatham." She pounds our table this time, her fist landing squarely in front of our now paralyzed client. "Lo and behold," she says, "we found Michelle Forrester's spare. In this man's garage."

A surge of commentary erupts in the gallery. The judge pounds his gavel, hard. Geraldine is on the move; she's got more.

"We also found a coil of clothesline hanging on a nail," she says, pointing at the evidence bag on the bench. "That clothesline."

Judge Long looks down at the rope, but doesn't react.

"We found blood on the garage floor," she says. "Traces, but enough."

The judge picks up the lab report again.

"That's right," Geraldine says as she watches him read. "It's a match."

She returns to her table. Clarence kneels beside it, retrieves a long, narrow, plastic-wrapped package, and hands it to her. It's almost as long as she is.

"And finally," she says, "we found this."

She lays it on the bench and returns to our table. "A shovel," she says, addressing the gallery. "The shovel that was used to murder Michelle Andrea Forrester."

The onlookers grow noisy again but Judge Long doesn't bother to hush them. Instead, he goes back to the lab report and the Kydd pushes a page from our copy across the table to me. He's highlighted the portion that details the evidence found on the underside of the shovel's heavy metal base: hair, blood, skin fragments. All Michelle's, along with a small slice of her scalp.

I lean toward my client, hoping he'll have something to say, some theory about what the hell happened here. He doesn't, though. He doesn't even seem to know I'm looking at him. He's turned completely around in his chair, his eyes locked with Honey's. She's staring back at him, dry-eyed, open-mouthed. She looks horrified. So does he. I'm willing to bet everyone else in the courtroom does too.

Judge Long sets the lab report on the bench, removes his glasses, and leans on his forearms. He's quiet for a moment—as is everyone else in the room now—staring down at the damning report. When he turns his attention our way, his somber expression says it all. Geraldine Schilling has done her job; she's assembled a case against the Senator, a real one. She's convinced the judge of that much, to say the least. "Counsel," he says to me, "how does your client plead?"

"Guilty." The voice is loud, definite, and it takes a split second for me to realize it came from the seat next to mine. The Senator is on his feet in a flash. I jump up and grab his arm. "Shut up," I tell him. "Now."

He shakes my hand away. "I'm ready for sentencing," he says to the startled judge. "I'm guilty."

The room goes nuts. Judge Long bangs his gavel a half dozen times. "Senator Kendrick," he says, "you're represented by counsel, sir. Your attorney will enter your plea. Please be seated."

It's obvious the Senator has no intention of doing any such thing. He moves out from behind our table, shaking his head at the judge. "My attorney doesn't know anything about it," he says. "I lied to her."

The noise in the gallery goes up another decibel.

"Look," he says to Judge Long, "Michelle Forrester and I had an affair."

Pandemonium erupts behind us.

"I broke it off," the Senator continues, "four months ago. But last Thursday . . ." He turns to Honey and grimaces. "I lapsed."

"Senator Kendrick," Judge Long says, almost shouting to be heard above the ruckus, "I strongly advise you to sit down now, sir. Your attorney is here to speak for you."

It's pretty clear the Senator isn't going to take the judge's advice. He's talking to everybody now. Everybody but the Kydd and me, that is. The spectators. The reporters. The District Attorney. "Michelle and I spent last Thursday night together," he says. "It was a terrible mistake."

"Senator!" The judge is on his feet now. He bangs his gavel once more, hard. "Please, sir, be seated."

Not a chance. "Michelle read more into that night than I ever intended," the Senator says. "She thought we'd reestablished our prior relationship. She thought we'd go forward as—well—as a couple." He pauses and stares at his wife for a few seconds. "Michelle wanted more from me than I was free to give."

Honey buries her face in her hands, sobbing. Abby wraps her arms around her mother, then she breaks down too.

"When I explained that to her," the Senator continues, "she got angry. She threatened to go to my wife, to tell her everything. And then . . ."

He pauses for a breath, and I realize for the first time that he's trembling.

"And then I lost my temper." He shrugs, exactly the way he did in my office when he described Michelle's impromptu visit to Old Harbor Road. *The rest was inevitable,* he's telling us.

I don't buy it.

"Your Honor," I shout above the ruckus, "we ask the court to enter a *not* guilty plea at this time."

"That's out of the question." Geraldine is shouting now too. It's the only way to be heard in here. "The man already entered a plea. He can't change it now."

Judge Gould bangs his gavel repeatedly until the crowd quiets. He doesn't speak until the silence is complete. "You forget, Ms. Schilling, that this man's plea is not entered until I accept it." His words are quiet, measured. "And I don't." He looks from Geraldine to me to the Senator. "I don't accept *any* plea at this time."

"But Your Honor—" Geraldine says.

He silences her with one hand, packs up his file, and stands.

The confused bailiff tells the spectators to rise. "We'll reconvene on Monday morning," the judge says as he leaves the bench, "first thing. The defendant will enter his plea at that time."

Geraldine shakes her head; she's frustrated. A guilty plea today would have been far more tidy.

Judge Long pauses at the chambers door and turns to the defense table. The Senator is still on his feet, in front of it, the Kydd now at his side. "Senator Kendrick," the judge says, "I suspect your lawyer plans to spend some time with you this weekend."

I sure as hell do. They both look at me and I nod to confirm it.

Judge Long turns his attention back to the still-trembling Senator. "I strongly suggest you listen to her, sir, take her advice." He takes another quick glance at me, then heads for chambers.

The room erupts again as soon as the judge exits. The guards head for their prisoner at once, but I step in front of them. "Give us a minute?" I ask. They nod and resume their posts against the side wall.

"What the hell was that?" I bark at my client.

"It was a confession," he says.

"It was not. It was an act. You were lying."

He shakes his head, his eyes angry. "You don't know what you're talking about," he says. "I was owning up to my crime."

"You were owning up to someone *else's* crime."

He takes a deep breath before he answers. "That's ridiculous," he says, his voice even. "But I understand. You're a criminal defense attorney. You're not used to people coming clean."

I get as close to him as I can without stepping on his feet. "What I'm not *used to*," I tell him, "is standing by while my client pleads guilty to a crime he didn't commit. And I don't intend to get used to it anytime soon."

He looks into the distance, grits his teeth, and says nothing.

"Listen to me," I tell him, "we're talking about first-degree murder here, life behind bars. Life. Whatever it is you're hiding can't be worse."

His gaze returns to me; it's steady. "You don't know that, Counselor," he says.

And he's right. I don't.

CHAPTER 26

Harry doesn't pull into our office driveway when we reach it; he cruises on by. We're eastbound on Main Street, destination undisclosed. "What?" I ask. "The day hasn't been long enough? We're taking a joyride now?"

"Just a short one," he says.

He's out of his mind. It's seven-thirty. He hung around the Superior Courthouse until six, when the Holliston jurors retired to their hotel for the evening, then he crossed the parking lot and caught the final moments of chaos in the District Court. It was pushing seven by the time we extricated ourselves from the reporters and spectators and made our way through the snowdrifts to his Jeep.

The Kydd pulled out of the county complex just moments

before we did, late for a hot date. *The story of my life,* he always says. If he's going to keep this job, he's fond of telling Harry and me, he may as well enter a Roman Catholic seminary. Harry always tells him to forget it. *Rectors don't cotton to Southern Baptists,* he says.

"Are stores open?" Harry asks now.

He really isn't of this planet. "It's eight days before Christmas," I tell him. "Of course they are."

"How about flower stores?" he asks.

I stare at him.

"Florists?" he says.

"I know what they're called, Harry. I'm trying to figure out why the hell you want to go flower shopping at this particular moment." My feet hurt, my head aches, and my stomach's growling. I want to sit someplace warm and quiet and eat dinner, not go shopping—for flowers or anything else.

He narrows his eyes, the way he always does when he's about to hand me a line. "Thought I'd pick up a little something for my special someone," he says.

That's a bald-faced lie; he thought nothing of the sort. He knows me well enough to know that at this point in the workweek, I'd rather have a back rub than a bouquet of roses. "Who is she?" I ask.

He laughs, then reaches for my hand and kisses it, a habit of his that always melts my heart. "You know who she is," he says.

"Well, she's out of luck," I tell him. "I don't think you'll find any florists open at this hour." I lean over and kiss his cheek. "But I bet she'd settle for a filet mignon and a good Cabernet."

"You read my mind," he says. "How about Pete's?"

Pete's is a celebrated steak house on Main Street in Chatham.

The entire menu is top-notch, but it's the baked stuffed potatoes that bring Harry to his knees. "Sounds good," I tell him. "There's just one problem."

"What's that?"

"You've already passed it."

"I know," he says, nodding. "We'll come back. I want to make a couple of stops first. Quick ones." He pulls into the parking lot of the Chatham Village Market, a first-class, employee-owned grocery store, and stops in front of the Christmas trees.

I'm surprised. Harry and I normally decorate a tree together, in my Windmill Lane cottage, on Christmas Eve. We've never bought one this early before. "What are you doing?" I ask.

"I need a wreath," he says. He hops out, leaves the Jeep running, and heads for the small shanty that serves as a temporary shop. His sudden concern with holiday decor leaves me mystified, to put it mildly. I watch while he chats with the tree merchant, a burly man in a fisherman's knit sweater, denim overalls, and a striped stocking cap. In no time at all, Harry's headed back, his purchase complete. He gestures for me to roll down my window, then hands me a fragrant circle of pine.

It's understated, lovely. Small, dark red berries are clustered in random spots around it and a single matching ribbon is tied in a simple bow on one side. "Where are you going to hang it?" I ask as Harry puts the Jeep back in gear.

"I'm not," he says. He turns right out of the driveway, heading eastbound again.

"Pete's is the other way," I remind him.

"One more stop," he says, covering my hand with his. "It'll just take a few minutes. Promise."

We ride in silence for a short while. Harry takes a left on Old

Harbor Road, then a right on Highland Avenue. I was mystified before, but I'm downright stunned now. "We're going to church?" I ask. "The *Catholic* church?"

He shakes his head as he parks on the street, just past the main entrance. "Hell, no," he says. "The steeple would implode if we did. I wouldn't do that to the good Catholics so close to Christmas."

Harry takes the wreath from my lap and gets out of the Jeep, so I follow. A few dozen cars are already parked in the church's large lot and more are pulling in. A lighted sign near the front steps explains. The children's Christmas pageant begins at eight, fifteen minutes from now. The organist has already begun, though. "O Come, All Ye Faithful" wafts through the air, growing louder each time a churchgoer opens the front doors. Harry sings along as we walk around the side of the church into complete darkness. *"Adeste, fideles, laeti triumphantes; Venite, venite in Bethlehem."*

He's full of surprises tonight. "You know the *Latin* version?" I ask.

"Natum videte Regem angelorum."

"All of it?"

"Venite adoremus, venite adoremus, venite adoremus, Dominum."

I stare at him, astonished. He shrugs and drapes his arm around my shoulders. "High school," he says. "The Jesuits gave me no choice."

Harry stops when we reach the back of the church and it takes a moment for my eyes to adjust to the total darkness. When they do, I realize we're in a small cemetery, the one Monsignor Davis described on the witness stand. Now I understand Harry's need for a wreath. There are about a dozen graves back here, situated randomly around a stone image of a woman clutching her heart. A crown of thorns is pressed onto her head, which I'm guessing goes a long way toward explaining her chest pain.

We locate Father McMahon's burial site easily; its headstone looks much newer than the others, even after a year in the elements. Harry sets the wreath at its base and the two of us stand in silence, staring at the grave of a man neither one of us ever met. His simple stone is inscribed with his full Christian name, his dates of birth and death, and a passage from scripture:

> *Come to Me, all you who labor and are burdened,*
> *and I will give you rest. Take My yoke upon*
> *you and learn from Me, for I am gentle and lowly*
> *in heart, and you will find rest for your souls.*
> *For My yoke is easy and My burden is light.*
> *Matthew 11:28–30.*

"It's a damned shame," Harry says. "Derrick Holliston murdered a good man. And then I murdered his memory."

"You were doing your job," I tell him. "You didn't have any other option."

Harry shakes his head. "Option or no option," he says, "my words maligned a man who didn't deserve it. I'm responsible for them."

"You don't know what happened here a year ago."

"Yes, I do," he says quietly.

Here we go again. "You don't, Harry. You have your suspicions, but you don't *know* anything about it. Maybe it went down just as Holliston said."

He arches his eyebrows at me, but says nothing. He doesn't need to. I'm a broken record. And he's not listening anymore.

"Christmas visitors!"

I jump a little before I realize it's Monsignor Davis coming through the darkness. He opens his arms, welcoming us, as he approaches. "As the Magi visited the Christ child in the manger, so you've come to visit our Father McMahon."

"Damn," Harry says, shaking the priest's hand. "We forgot the frankincense. And the shops are plum out of myrrh."

The Monsignor laughs. "Not to worry," he says. "Frank was never one to covet worldly wealth. He'd be glad just for your visit."

"Don't be so sure about that," Harry says. "If I were Frank, I wouldn't offer me an eggnog."

Monsignor Davis looks curious, but apparently decides not to inquire further. "Any word from the jury?" he asks instead.

"Nada," Harry tells him. "They've quit for the night. They'll be back at work by eight tomorrow."

The Monsignor checks his watch, then heads for the church's back door. "The pageant's just about to begin," he says. "Are you coming?"

Harry starts to laugh, then catches himself. "Maybe some other time," he says. "The camels are hungry."

The Monsignor waves and then turns away from us, laughing as the heavy door slams shut behind him.

Harry drapes his arm around my shoulders again as we head back toward Old Harbor Road. "Who're you calling a camel?" I ask.

He lowers his head, his expression hangdog. "I knew *that* was a mistake." He smiles apologetically, looks a bit abashed, even, but by the time we reach the Jeep, he's whistling "Midnight at the Oasis."

If we were to continue in the same direction on Old Harbor Road, we'd eventually come upon the Kendrick estate, where I suspect Honey and Abby are in hiding tonight—from the persistent press; from well-intentioned neighbors; from the prying public. We don't, though. Harry makes a U-turn instead, heading for Pete's, and in the dim glow of the streetlights, he looks a little bit sad.

"Remember," I tell him, "even if you're right about Holliston, you don't have a monopoly on lying clients. I've got one on my hands too."

"So you said." He reaches over and cups my cheek in his palm, another habit of his that warms my heart. "What makes you so sure?" he asks.

It's a rational question; I wish I had a better answer. "I don't know," I tell him. "But I am. Charles Kendrick is lying. He's taking the rap for a murder he didn't commit."

"You don't know that," Harry says. "You can't."

He's right, of course. I can't.

But I do.

CHAPTER 27

Saturday, December 18

Saturday mornings in our office tend to be busy, particularly for the Kydd. He handles most of the misdemeanors that come our way, and Friday nights—particularly the cold, dark ones—seem to foster misdemeanor mania. He has a full lineup this morning: all the usual suspects and a handful of new recruits. Minor drug busts, barroom brawls, and petty thefts fill our front office, the Kydd meeting with each of the accused in the conference room, first come, first served. The more serious cases—the ones that warrant weekend lockup—won't surface until Monday morning.

Harry and I pour mugs of coffee, then head upstairs to my office. Neither of us expects to get much work done today—we're worn out from the week's events—but we need to be here, ready to race to the courthouse, in case the Holliston jury reaches a decision. Generally speaking, jurors don't like weekend duty, and they don't like *any* duty a week before Christmas. A quick determination of Derrick Holliston's fate wouldn't surprise either of us.

Harry sets his mug on the coffee table and flops on the couch. I take a seat at my desk, figuring I'll sort through the week's phone messages and mail, then tackle the pile of pleadings our dutiful associate has stacked neatly on my credenza. The intercom buzzes before I get started, though, and I'm surprised. I didn't think the Kydd would come up for air for another few hours. "Marty," he says, "there's someone here to see you. Her name's Helene Wilson. She says you're not expecting her, but it'll just take a few minutes."

"Send her up," I tell him. Harry arches his eyebrows at me; we didn't anticipate company.

She appears at the top of the spiral staircase in a red cable-knit sweater and blue jeans; the Kydd must have already taken her coat. "I'm sorry to show up unannounced," she says. "I was planning to make an appointment on Monday, but I was driving by and saw all the cars parked outside and I thought maybe you were here, even though it's Saturday. And then I thought maybe I *shouldn't* wait until Monday."

She's worked up, speaking quickly, her cheeks flushed. I rummage around on my desk to find a legal pad and pen, then write: *It's fine. I'm glad to see you.* If Senator Kendrick's next-door neighbor has something additional to say, I want to hear it now, not later.

Harry's on his feet and I make the introductions, hers out loud, his on paper. They both sit, side by side on the couch, and I grab a chair from in front of my desk and face them, my eyes on Helene, my legal pad and pen at the ready.

"I saw Senator Kendrick's arraignment," she says. "I was there, in the courthouse, yesterday."

Of course she was. I noticed her before we got started; I noticed her troubled eyes. But I didn't see her—or anyone else, for that matter—in the frenzied blur that followed.

"I also watched it on the eleven o'clock news last night," she says. "The reporter described it as nothing short of a circus. I have to admit I agreed with him."

No argument here. I wait while Helene seems to search, struggle even, for her next words.

"Is he sticking to it?" she asks at last. "Is the Senator still claiming he killed the young woman?"

I nod again, though I'm aware that if Charles Kendrick had changed his mind during the last twelve hours, I'd probably be the last to know.

She presses one hand to her neck and shakes her head. Again her eyes are worried, her expression distressed. "Something is terribly wrong," she says.

I lean forward, closer to her. Harry eyes her carefully too. *Why do you say that?* I scribble.

"Because Michelle Forrester was alive and well when she left the Senator's home on Friday morning," she says. "I saw her leave. It was her car. I *saw* it." She points at her eyes, as if she thinks I might not trust that *other* sense of hers. She's wrong, though; I do. I trust all of Helene Wilson's senses.

Harry reaches for the pen and paper. He looks bothered, maybe even skeptical. *The BMW roadster is a popular car,* he writes. *Maybe it's a coincidence; maybe a different roadster happened down your lane that morning, then turned around when the driver realized it's a dead end.*

She shakes her head before he puts the pen down. "No," she insists, "it wasn't. They showed *her* BMW roadster on the news last night. And they reported for the first time that it has a silk rose attached to the antenna, a yellow one. *That* was the car I saw, fake flower and all."

Harry and I are quiet as we absorb this information. Neither of us watched the news last night. By the time we were finished with dinner at Pete's, we were both having trouble keeping our eyes open. Harry even considered passing on dessert, but the crème brûlée brought him to his senses.

The intercom buzzes yet again and it takes me a moment to react. It squawks three times before I answer, and I can hear the frustration in the Kydd's breathing even before he speaks. He's right; we do need a secretary. He's doing way too many things at once, a well-known recipe for malpractice. "What is it?" I ask, still staring at Helene.

"Big Red called," he says. "The jury's done. You guys have a verdict."

CHAPTER 28

Weekend verdicts tend to slip beneath the public's radar screen—at least until the following Monday. Most journalists and courtroom aficionados are at home with their families on weekends, tending to household chores, watching their sons and daughters play the season's sports, or, at this time of year, trimming a tree. So I expected the parking lot to be relatively empty when Harry and I pulled into the county complex in his Jeep on this snowy Saturday. I was wrong.

Like the lot, the main courtroom in the Superior Courthouse is packed. Big Red is the only bailiff on duty and he's got his hands full. The county will cough up time-and-a-half for his services today, just as it will for our stenographer and Dottie Bearse. All three of them will earn every last penny of it, none more so than

Big Red. The benches and aisles are already full, so he props open the rear double doors. The overflow crowd can watch from the hallway, though it's unlikely they'll hear anything at that distance. He can't send them downstairs to the conference room on a Saturday. There's no staff on duty to monitor the room, no technician to record the proceedings.

Geraldine and Clarence are seated at their table, their demeanors decidedly different than they were forty-eight hours ago. The defendant's conviction looked like a slam dunk then. It doesn't at the moment. And even if they pull it off—even if the jurors agree with Geraldine that her office's failure to disclose the disappearance of the monstrance doesn't amount to a hill of beans—the appeal will be a nightmare. Geraldine looks stressed. Clarence looks much worse.

The side door opens and two guards usher Derrick Holliston to our table. He's neatly groomed, as he has been throughout trial, and he seems completely composed, at ease, as if whatever is about to happen in this room is of little consequence to him. He pauses when he reaches the table, staring at something behind me, and I turn to find out what's caught his attention. It's Bobby the Butcher—and Monsignor Davis—side by side in the front row behind our table.

"Sit down," I tell Holliston. "Turn the hell around and sit down."

He does, but he takes his time about it, sneering at the two before he complies. When I check on them again, their eyes say it all. The Monsignor would like to save Holliston's soul. The Butcher would like to wring his neck.

The two jurors who were informed they were alternates at the close of the case yesterday are here too, chatting in the front row behind Geraldine's table. One is a twenty-five-year-old landscaper who paid particularly keen attention throughout the trial. He seemed genuinely disappointed to learn he wouldn't get to deliberate with the others. His companion is Maria Marzetti's admirer from the back row. I suspect his presence here is only partially attributable to his interest in the case.

Harry plants his elbows on the table, his head in his hands. He looks far more worried than Holliston does. His isn't the usual defense attorney's concern, though. The jurors in this case have four choices, four potential verdicts, as is true in most first-degree-murder trials. And Harry's not sure which one of them worries him most.

In all murder cases, the judge is obligated to instruct the jury on every lesser-included offense that might be supported by the evidence. Case law is clear that an instruction is required where *any view* of the evidence would support the lesser-included result. As a practical matter, this means most murder juries are asked to choose from among first-degree, second-degree, and manslaughter charges. The fourth option, of course—available only if the jurors believe Holliston acted to preserve his own life—is an outright acquittal.

Geraldine argued yesterday that a manslaughter instruction shouldn't be given in this case. No view of the evidence would support such a result, she said. Giving an instruction on it would do nothing more than invite a compromise verdict. And *not* giving the instruction would actually *benefit* the defendant, she claimed. If the jurors fail to find the required elements of second-degree murder, they'll have no choice but to acquit.

Our District Attorney's argument was a loser. Voluntary manslaughter is defined as an unlawful killing with intent to kill, but without malice. The statute specifically provides that a killing is done "without malice" if it results from an excessive use of force during self-defense or if it occurs in the heat of passion caused by reasonable provocation. Technically, at least, the jury could be justified in finding either of those scenarios in Holliston's case.

Judge Gould didn't buy Geraldine's pitch from the outset, but he actually laughed when she purported to have the defendant's best interests at heart. "We're not in Las Vegas, Ms. Schilling," he said, "and this court is not a casino. We're not here to force the defendant to roll the dice and then live with his losses." That was the end of the argument. And Harry never said a word.

Big Red calls us to our feet as the chambers door opens and Judge Gould strides quickly to the bench. He's in his robe, business as usual, but today his shirt collar is unbuttoned beneath it, the absence of a tie his only nod to Saturday. "Bring them in," he says as he sits, and Big Red heads for the side door. Holliston watches him leave, then looks down at the table and shakes his head. "I still don't like that guy," he mutters.

"Rumor has it he doesn't think a hell of a lot of you, either," I tell him.

That notion seems to strike our hotheaded client as preposterous; he bolts upright and glares at me. I feel a sudden relief about reaching the end of the road in this case, no matter what the verdict might be. I'm tired of Derrick John Holliston. And I've had more than enough of his angry eyes.

Big Red returns in seconds, the jurors filing into the courtroom behind him in complete silence. Most of them avert their eyes—they look at their hands, the clock, the floor—as they take their seats in the box. Not all, though. Robert Eastman and Alex Doane stare directly at us—at Holliston, in fact—as soon as they enter the

212

room. Maria Marzetti does too. I scan the panel quickly, searching for the telltale white paper, and it takes only a few seconds for me to spot it. Gregory Harmon clutches the form in his right hand. It's the verdict slip; the one guy Harry would have kept off the panel had Holliston not called the shots is our foreman. He stares straight ahead as he sits; his expression reveals nothing.

Judge Gould bids the jurors good morning as they take their seats and they all return the sentiment. He nods to our table and Harry and I get to our feet. Holliston takes his time joining us, as if this is our moment of truth, not his. The guards who ushered him into the courtroom have been standing near his chair since they got here, but they inch closer to it now, their readiness palpable.

The judge pauses to allow Dottie Bearse to recite the docket number and then he turns back to the panel. "Ladies and gentlemen," he says, "have you reached a verdict?"

Gregory Harmon stands. "We have, Your Honor." His eleven compatriots remain seated, nodding in agreement. There's not a sound in the room. If the spectators are breathing, they're doing it on the sly.

Big Red hustles to the jury box, retrieves the verdict slip from Gregory Harmon, and ferries it across the courtroom to the bench. Judge Gould reads in silence, his expression a well-rehearsed neutral.

The judge passes the form back to Big Red, then turns to Dottie again. This time she stands at her desk. "Mr. Foreman," she says, "in the matter of *The Commonwealth of Massachusetts versus Derrick John Holliston,* on the charge of murder in the first degree, murder committed with extreme atrocity or cruelty, what say you?"

Holliston drums his fingers on the table. He's impatient; it seems he's got other matters to attend to. I step on his foot, hard. He glares at me yet again, but at least he stops drumming.

Big Red returns the verdict slip to Gregory Harmon and the foreman opens it to read. He doesn't need to do that, of course; he knows what it says. "On the charge of murder in the first degree," he intones, "we find the defendant, Derrick John Holliston, not guilty."

The courtroom erupts. More than a few of the spectators shout angry criticisms at the jurors. An even greater number actually *boo*. The Barnstable County Superior Courthouse sounds like Fenway Park during a Derek Jeter at-bat.

Judge Gould bangs his gavel repeatedly, but it has little effect. Holliston turns around and half sits on our table, a small smile spreading across his lips. I turn too, to take in the scene. Most of the spectators are on their feet, and more than a few of the shouters have their fists in the air. Big Red hurries down the center aisle, pulling the worst offenders from the benches, steering them toward the back doors. He's having a hard time ejecting them, though. The overflow crowd has the exit blocked.

The judge is on his feet now too, his gavel working like a jackhammer. He calls for quiet repeatedly, and the free-for-all settles down a bit after a half dozen of his pleas. "We'll sit here all day," he shouts, "and we'll eject every last one of you, if that's what it takes to restore order."

Holliston lets out a little laugh beside me; he's enjoying this.

Monsignor Davis isn't. He and the Butcher may be the only two people in the room who are still in their seats. The Monsignor's eyes are closed, his head bowed and his lips moving rapidly. Silent prayers, I presume, for everyone in this courtroom. The Butcher's eyes are closed too—they're squeezed shut, in fact—and his fists are clenched. I'm glad he's not standing in either of the side aisles.

If there were a wall anywhere close to him, I'm pretty sure he'd punch a hole in it. Whatever modicum of confidence he may have had left in our judicial system after his own ordeal with Derrick Holliston has just gone up in smoke.

Big Red has managed to part the lobby crowd, creating a path by which his dozen or so worst offenders can exit. The noise level drops a notch once they're gone, but the judge keeps hammering. "Quiet," he shouts, "this instant." And this time, for some reason, he gets it.

"Another outburst like that," he says, still catching his breath as he sits, "and we will empty the gallery." He waits, letting his words sink in, like an angry parent threatening to ground a wayward teenager. "Ms. Bearse," he says at last, "you may proceed."

Generally speaking, the courtroom is not a place for the weak-kneed. Even Dottie Bearse, who's spent her entire adult life working in this arena, looks shaken. She pours a glass of water at her desk and takes a long drink. Her face has gone pale and her hands are trembling. "Mr. Foreman," she says, her voice noticeably quieter than it was a few minutes ago, "in the matter of *The Commonwealth of Massachusetts versus Derrick John Holliston,* on the charge of murder in the second degree, murder committed with malice, but without deliberate premeditation or extreme atrocity and cruelty, what say you?"

Gregory Harmon swallows hard as he opens the verdict slip to read again. The document is merely a crutch, of course. If he keeps his gaze fixed on the written word, he avoids the possibility of eye contact with the man whose fate he's pronouncing. At least two of his fellow jurors don't seem to need any such device. Robert Eastman and Alex Doane haven't stopped staring at Holliston since they got here.

"On the charge of murder in the second degree," Gregory Harmon recites, "we find the defendant, Derrick John Holliston . . ." The foreman pauses and, much to my surprise, he looks up, directly at Holliston. "*Not* guilty."

Maybe it's due to the effectiveness of Judge Gould's threats. Or maybe the spectators used up their outrage when the murder-one verdict was announced. Whatever the reason, the courtroom at this moment is still, silent.

The judge seems surprised by the quiet too. He has his gavel in hand, but he doesn't need it. "Ms. Bearse," he says, "you may proceed."

"Mr. Foreman," Dottie says, "in the matter of *The Commonwealth of Massachusetts versus Derrick John Holliston,* on the charge of voluntary manslaughter, a killing with intent but without malice, done either through an excessive use of force in self-defense or in the heat of passion caused by reasonable provocation, what say you?"

Gregory Harmon is still looking directly at Holliston. He doesn't bother to read from the verdict slip this time. "On the charge of voluntary manslaughter," he says quietly, "we find the defendant, Derrick John Holliston . . ."

He drops his hands to his sides, the verdict slip folded in two, cupped in one palm. His eyes are still fixed on our client. And his gaze is steady.

"Guilty."

Holliston's up. The guards lunge for him at once, but they're not fast enough. His chair topples backward to the floor. Our table flips over in the other direction. And then all hell breaks loose. The crowd is in an uproar.

"This is bogus!" Holliston screams over the din. The guards

tackle him and within seconds, they have him out flat on the carpet, on his stomach, cuffed and shackled. He's still screaming, though, struggling against the thick arms that restrain him, trying to be heard above the angry mob in the gallery. "Bogus!" he yells at the panel again. "You people don't get it," he screams. "That priest attacked me! This ain't nothin' but bogus!"

Again, Derrick Holliston's legal analysis is lacking. The verdict *isn't* bogus. In many ways, it's entirely consistent with *his* version of events. The crime-scene photographs have *excessive force* written all over them.

Holliston staggers when the guards yank him to his feet, the shackles preventing him from finding a natural stance. His wrists are cuffed behind his back, so he points at Harry the only way he can, with his chin. "Defective assistance of counsel," he shouts at Judge Gould. "That's what we got here. Defective assistance of counsel."

"Ineffective," Harry tells him.

Holliston looks perplexed; he actually shuts up for a few seconds.

"The word's *ineffective*," Harry explains. "It's *ineffective* assistance of counsel."

"There, you see?" Holliston says to the judge. "He admits it."

"Call for the colloquy, Your Honor," Harry says.

The colloquy is a ritual employed for the recording of verdicts in criminal cases in the Commonwealth. It occurs after the foreperson announces the verdict in open court and the clerk marks it on the indictment form. Though not required by any published rule or statute, well-established case law mandates the use of the colloquy in all criminal cases. In a vehicular-homicide case that Harry and I tried together last year, a juror suffered a heart attack and died after the verdict was returned, but before the colloquy was conducted. On appeal, Harry argued that the affirmation of the other eleven jurors was insufficient to sustain the guilty verdict. He won, the appellate court agreeing with his claim that a valid verdict can be rendered only by the final concurrence of twelve jurors.

We're in no shape to begin the colloquy at the moment, of course. Our table is still on its side, files and papers strewn across the carpeted floor, soggy from the contents of the now empty water pitcher. But Harry wants to call for the process quickly, at least, before Holliston gets himself ejected from the courtroom.

Judge Gould doesn't respond to Harry's request; he turns to our client instead. "Mr. Holliston," he says, "I am loathe to prevent any criminal defendant from witnessing every moment of his trial."

One of the guards moves Holliston out of the way as if he's a dog on a lead, while the other helps Big Red right the table. Harry joins them in picking up the mess.

"But mark my words, sir," the judge continues, "I will have you removed from this courtroom forthwith if you cause any further disruption."

The guard points Holliston to his now upright chair and he shuffles toward it, his face red, his eyes furious, the judge's admonition apparently of no concern.

Judge Gould takes a deep breath and looks out into the gallery. It's quiet now; the spectators seem to have been shocked back into silence when the furniture flew. "Ms. Bearse," he says, "you may begin."

Dottie stands, looking even more unnerved than she did after the first melee. "Mr. Foreman," she says, "and members of the jury, harken to your verdicts. On your oath, you do say that on the indictment for voluntary manslaughter, Derrick John Holliston is guilty, so say you, Mr. Foreman?"

Gregory Harmon has been on his feet this entire time. "Yes," he says. "I do."

Dottie looks to the other members of the panel. "So say you all?"

Eleven heads nod. "Yes," they say in unison.

Harry's up. "Call for a poll," he says.

Harry calls for a jury poll after every guilty verdict, regardless of how clear the jurors' answers are during the colloquy. In essence, the poll asks the same questions the colloquy does, but it puts the matter to each juror individually. Though it's unlikely any of them will change the answer, even a slight hesitation can fuel a flurry of post-trial motions and appellate arguments. Harry says it's malpractice for a defender to fail to call for a poll, and I think he's right.

"Mr. Harmon," Dottie begins, "is this your verdict?"

"It is," he answers.

"And is it the unanimous verdict of this jury?"

"Yes," he says as he sits.

"Mrs. Rowlands," Dottie continues, "is this your verdict?"

"Yes," she says. "That's my verdict."

"And is it the unanimous verdict of this jury?"

"It most certainly is," Cora replies.

Dottie continues through the front row of the jury box, putting the same pair of questions to each juror, getting the same pair of responses in return. Holliston doesn't react until Maria Marzetti delivers her double affirmative. "I *told* you she was a cat-lick," he mutters.

"Your powers of perception are staggering," I tell him.

219

He nods. At last we agree on something.

Geraldine leaves her chair and walks toward our table while Dottie Bearse continues the poll. It's not any of us the District Attorney is interested in, though. She walks behind Harry's chair, keeping her distance from Holliston, and leans over the bar. "I'm sorry," she says to Monsignor Davis.

"Don't be," he tells her. "It's enough. Mr. Holliston will have plenty of time to reflect upon his wrongdoing. Maybe he'll even ask the good Lord for forgiveness. Father McMahon wouldn't have wanted anything more."

Holliston snorts beside me and I elbow him. Geraldine glares at both of us. "Maybe not," she says to the Monsignor, "but I sure as hell did."

I'm sure she did. But overall, I believe Geraldine Schilling is relieved. Holliston isn't going to walk, after all. With a different jury, a panel more offended by prosecutorial misconduct, he may have. I'm pretty sure Harry is relieved for the same reason.

Dottie wraps up the poll, eliciting twenty-four affirmatives in all, none the least bit hesitant, none uncertain in any way. Judge Gould thanks her when she finishes and then turns to the panel. "Ladies and gentlemen," he says, "I extend the county's sincere thanks to each and every one of you. Jury service is vital to our system, essential to the preservation of a free society. You have served well."

"My ass," Holliston says. I should stomp on his foot again, but I don't bother.

"Now before you go," the judge continues, "I warn you that the attorneys in this case—at least some of them—will try to speak with you before you leave the courthouse. And although they were prohibited from having any direct contact with you while the case was ongoing, it's perfectly appropriate for them to do so now. They'll undoubtedly want to know what evidence you found persuasive, what issues were key to your decision. You're free to converse with them if you so choose, but you're under no obligation to do so. As of this moment, your service is complete. You're free to go. And you take with you the sincere thanks of this court."

With that, Big Red leads his charges back to the jury room to retrieve coats, hats, and other personal belongings. Harry gives me the eye and I head for the back doors, Clarence Wexler just a few steps behind me. Harry will stay here, in the courtroom, to make post-trial motions, and Geraldine will stay to oppose them. Harry will move for judgment notwithstanding the verdict and, when he loses that one, he'll move for a new trial. These motions are argued routinely after guilty verdicts are returned. And just as routinely, they're denied. While that's going on, I'll try to corner as many jurors as I can. So will Clarence.

Gregory Harmon and Cora Rowlands are the first to appear in the hallway, Robert Eastman and Alex Doane right behind them. I approach them and they stop as a group, seemingly willing to chat for a few minutes, at least. "Excessive force?" I ask. "Is that what you hung your hat on?"

Gregory Harmon nods as the other three turn to him, giving him the floor. Once the foreman, always the foreman. "Pretty much," he says. He seems uncomfortable, though.

Clarence snags the next group that emerges from the jury room and he ushers the three of them away from us, to the other side of the corridor. If they're going to tell him his screw-up with the monstrance was significant, he doesn't want me—or any other member of the bar—within earshot.

"Does that mean you believe Mr. Holliston's version of

events?" I ask my foursome. "Do you believe Father McMahon attacked him first?"

They exchange knowing glances but no one answers. I wait, surprised that the question is so difficult. "Not exactly," Harmon says at last.

"What then?"

"Excessive force is what we hung our hat on," he says. "It's not really what we believe."

I'm confused. Their expressions tell me it shows.

"We don't believe Father McMahon attacked that young man," Cora Rowlands says. "We don't even think the priest made advances. We just couldn't say, beyond a reasonable doubt, that he *didn't*."

Four more jurors come through the doorway and hurry past us, their downcast eyes saying they aren't interested in participating in our discussion; they can't get out of the courthouse fast enough.

"But if you couldn't say *that* beyond a reasonable doubt," I ask my group, "didn't you feel you should acquit?" That's sure as hell what the judge told them to do. He specifically instructed them that they should acquit Mr. Holliston unless the Commonwealth proved, beyond a reasonable doubt, that he did not act in self-defense.

They all shake their heads. "No way," Alex Doane says. "After what he did to Father McMahon, to another human being? No way were we putting him back on the street."

The jury room door opens again, and Maria Marzetti joins us. Alex Doane and Robert Eastman part to make room for her and then Eastman points toward the courtroom. "There's a lot of anger in that young man," he says.

He's right about that, of course. But the last time I checked, harboring anger wasn't a punishable offense on the Common-wealth's penal code. I can't help feeling that Harry and I short-changed Derrick Holliston somehow. Gregory Harmon seems to read my mind. "You and your partner did a good job," he says, "but you had one lousy client to work with."

Cora Rowlands nods in agreement. "He's trouble," she adds, "that much is clear."

"Let me make sure I have this straight," I tell them. "You couldn't find beyond a reasonable doubt that Holliston *didn't* act in self-defense, but you convicted him of manslaughter anyway?"

They all look at one another before nodding at me. "That's what we did," Gregory Harmon says, "and we justified it with the excessive-force provision. But the bottom line is—that guy needs to go to jail. No way he should be walking the streets."

With that, four of them leave. Maria Marzetti hangs back, though. She says nothing, keeps her eyes on the hallway floor, until her cohorts are out of sight. "Listen," she says when she finally looks up at me, "I'm not particularly proud of the route we took, but in my heart, I believe justice was served here."

I shake my head at her. "Were the judge's instructions unclear?"

"Not at all," she says. "As far as they went, they were perfectly clear. But we didn't feel they went far enough. We didn't feel they really covered this situation."

I lean against the wall, wondering why we bother to give jury instructions in the first place.

"Sometimes you have to trust your gut," Maria adds. "And in the end, that's what the twelve of us did." She gives me a small smile, an almost apologetic one, and then heads down the hallway.

"Maria!" It's her back-row admirer, emerging from the court-room with the rest of the spectators. Harry's post-trial motions were denied even faster than usual, it seems. She stops and turns around at the sound of her name and her newfound friend pulls ahead of the crowd, hurrying in her direction. She seems happy to see him. Maybe something positive will result from this fiasco of a trial after all.

I take my time heading back to the courtroom, Maria's words hot on my brain. *Sometimes you have to trust your gut.* I agree with her; I'm a great proponent of trusting one's gut. It's on that basis alone that I'm going to deliver a stern lecture to Senator Kendrick when we're through here. Maybe his overnight in the House of Correction has instilled some sense in him; maybe now I'll be able to persuade him to enter a not guilty plea on Monday morning.

Harry and I discussed Senator Kendrick's case at length during dinner last night. Harry pointed out that the Senator seemed to know something terrible had happened to Michelle Forrester on Wednesday—when he showed up in my office to confess to having been with her the night before she disappeared—even though her body wasn't discovered until the next day. I'd thought of that too, of course, but I had no explanation to offer. "Charles Kendrick almost certainly knows more than he's saying," I told Harry. "That's been a given with him from the get-go. But he didn't kill Michelle. I'm certain of that."

My unsubstantiated certainty seemed to be enough for Harry. "Then talk him out of his kamikaze plea," he said, "before it's too late."

The courtroom is all but empty when I return. The benches are cleared and Derrick Holliston has been carted away. Judge Gould is still on the bench, though, with Geraldine and Harry engaged in some last-minute haggling before him. I head toward our table, intending to sit, but a sudden realization stops me. Senator Kendrick *did* know something terrible had happened to Michelle on Wednesday. He knows a hell of a lot more than he's saying. And now I know too.

"Excuse me, Your Honor." I change direction and head for the bench instead.

Judge Gould and Harry both look surprised. Geraldine looks annoyed. She was midsentence when I interrupted.

"I'm sorry," I tell them all. "But I need your car keys, Harry."

He looks at me as if I've lost my mind. We're forty miles from Chatham; he doesn't like the idea of walking home in the snow.

"I'll come back for you, Harry. But give me the keys. Now. I have to go this instant."

CHAPTER 29

"You caught them again," I say quietly. "It was bad enough the first time, at the apartment in Boston, but this was more than you could bear. After his pleading. After his promises. After you took him back."

Honey Kendrick is a better actress than I would have guessed. If I didn't know better, I'd think she was really in the dark, clueless about what I'm saying. We're at the scene of the crime—her dormered, three-car garage—in the bay closest to the house. I've heard it said that murderers always return to the scene. This time, at least, it's proved true. She was in here when I pulled up in Harry's Jeep, standing perfectly still, staring at the vacant spot where Michelle Forrester's car would have been.

"You arrived last Thursday night," I continue, "not Friday.

You got here the night of your husband's press conference at Four Cs. Maybe you thought you'd surprise him, take him out for a nice dinner."

She stares at me, her eyes wide.

"But he's not the one who got the surprise, is he? Maybe you parked here, in the garage, and recognized her car. Or maybe you stopped in the driveway, went inside, and heard them. Either way, you caught them again."

Honey stares at the floor, says nothing.

"So you waited." I point to a wooden staircase leading to the second story, then up to the rafters. "Those dormers, they accommodate a spare bedroom, don't they? Maybe even a small in-law apartment?"

She nods and tears up all at once.

"You waited there, probably, until morning. My guess is you didn't sleep."

She bites her bottom lip and her tears spill over.

"You didn't plan it. You'd never plan such a thing."

She shakes her head.

"But when you saw her the next morning—young, full of promise, and radiant after a night with *your* husband—something snapped. You wanted to hurt her. You wanted her to ache every bit as much as you did."

The door at the top of the staircase opens. Abby emerges, walks down a couple of steps and stands still, staring at us. She's obviously been listening; her face is ashen. I won't stop, though. I can't now.

"So you reached for something—anything—you could use to make her hurt. It turned out to be the shovel. And in a split second, without any forethought, you swung. Once."

"With a strength you never knew you had."

The words are calm, steady. And they're coming from Abby's mouth.

I'm uncertain for a moment, unsure what to make of her comment. And then—in a heartbeat—I'm not. Honey Kendrick *doesn't* know the details. Abby does.

Her mother is a step ahead of me. "Abigail," she says, her voice trembling, "be quiet this instant."

Abigail doesn't seem to hear. "And then," she says, "even though you've never seen a dead person before, you know you're looking at one. You're as sure of it as you are of your own name."

She walks toward us, down the stairs, her cheeks tear-streaked. "And then you panic—like you've never panicked before. You can't move at first, you're paralyzed, and then you can't *stop* moving. You have to get rid of her somehow. Her and her car. And her stupid car is so small she won't fit in the trunk. But you can't drive down the road with her in the passenger seat. It's starting to get light. And she's a mess."

"Abigail, you're talking nonsense," her mother tries. She's wrong, though. Abigail is telling the truth. It's written on her face.

She stops at the bottom of the steps, looks at her mother, then at me. "So you take out the spare," she says.

She's on autopilot. Her mother can't change the course. No one can.

"And somehow you get her into the trunk, then, but it still won't shut. So you find a piece of clothesline and you tie it."

"Abigail, please," Honey says, "stop." Her words are flat, though. Even she knows it's too late. Abigail can't stop.

"And then you dump her into Pleasant Bay because she's already dead and there's nothing you can do about it. And you know somebody's going to find her, but you feel sort of lucky because the tide's going out, so maybe it'll take a while, and all you really want is time to think."

Honey backs up to the wall, slumps against it.

"And then you leave the stupid car in the woods. And you know somebody's going to find that, too, but you don't know what else to do."

Abby pauses to breathe. She isn't pale anymore; she's flushed from the base of her neck up, dark red blotches on both cheeks.

"And then your father gets arrested for it," she says. "And at first you think that's not so bad, because he *didn't* do it, so he'll get off."

If only it were that simple.

"But then he goes and pleads guilty and you don't know what's going on. Until he stares at your mom that way. And then you do."

She looks me square in the eyes and waits. She seems to think I might say it for her. She's wrong. I won't.

"He thinks *she* did it," she says at last, pointing at her mother. "Just what you thought. And he's going to take the blame for her, go to jail for her, give up everything for her. *That's* how much he loves her. More than he ever loved that *girl*." She points at the empty parking spot, as if Michelle is still here.

And she is. For the Kendricks, all three of them, Michelle Forrester will always be here.

Chapter 30

A Week Later

Harry's second-floor apartment is empty, the fireplace cold. I'm surprised at first, but after a moment I realize I shouldn't be. I have a pretty good hunch where he's gone on this Christmas morning. I back the Thunderbird out of the office driveway and head toward St. Veronica's in the steadily falling snow. The day's first light is on the horizon, muted by silver-gray cloud cover.

When Luke was little, he couldn't bolt out of his bed fast enough on Christmas mornings. He'd burst into my bedroom well before dawn, Danny Boy hot on his heels, the two of them panting with excitement. They'd both tug at my blankets and pajamas until I opened my reluctant eyes, and then Luke would complain—and Danny Boy would whimper—about the unbearable length of time it took for me to find my robe and negotiate the stairs. Those days are long gone, of course. Luke and Danny Boy were sound asleep—both snoring—when I left our Windmill Lane cottage twenty minutes ago. Sleeping in is a luxury Luke will enjoy only for another couple of weeks. Classes resume in early January.

Abby Kendrick's won't, though. She may return to the hallowed halls of Harvard someday—her father has vowed she will—but it won't be anytime soon. Geraldine Schilling offered her a better-than-decent plea bargain—a reduction to involuntary manslaughter, a dismissal of the obstruction of justice charges, and a recommendation to the court for leniency in sentencing—all in exchange for a full written confession, and all with the blessings of the Forrester family. On the sage advice of veteran defender Bert Saunders, Abby took it.

She was arraigned and sentenced in a solitary proceeding—yet another media feeding frenzy—on Wednesday morning, just forty-eight hours after all charges against her father were dismissed. Judge Leon Long took Geraldine's leniency recommendation to heart. He gave Abby six-to-eight, a decidedly light term under current statutory guidelines. With good behavior and a little luck, she'll be out in five.

Our system worked for Abby Kendrick—not a claim every criminal defendant can make. It worked in part because our District Attorney recognized a critical fact: Abby's crime—though undeniably heinous—was born of passion, a circumstance we, as a society, have long recognized as a mitigating factor. It also worked because her case ended up on the docket of Leon Long, a man who carries a hefty dose of compassion into the courtroom—and up to the bench—every day of his working life. And for that she has her father to thank. It's unlikely Judge Long would have been summoned to serve had the initial arraignee not been the Commonwealth's senior senator.

Honey headed to San Francisco, to stay with her parents for a while, as soon as the sheriff's patrol car left the Barnstable County Complex with her only child in the caged backseat. She told her husband to expect the process server on his doorstep—with her Petition for Divorce in hand—within the week. Charles Kendrick says he won't contest it, and he won't try to talk her out of it. He doesn't plan to fight for his long-held seat in the U.S. Senate, either; he simply doesn't have any fight left in him. The public outcry for his resignation began the day he was charged with Michelle Forrester's murder. It diminished only slightly when the truth emerged.

It wasn't until Honey pulled out of the county complex on Wednesday that I noticed Luke's truck idling in the driveway, a few spaces behind where her car had been parked, a half dozen spots from where the sheriff's patrol car had been. There were tears on his cheeks when I started walking toward him, but he was quick to brush them away before rolling down his window. "She'll be okay," he said right away, as if I were the one in need of reassurance. "Abby's strong," he added. "She'll get through this."

Generally speaking, I'm proud of my son. But at that moment, my maternal pride hit an all-time high. I hope Luke never loses his generous spirit toward others. I hope he'll always be as fiercely loyal to his friends as he is today. And as to Abby Kendrick, I also hope he's right.

Harry's Jeep is parked on the street, in front of the chapel's main entrance. I pull in behind it and cut the engine, then walk around the stone building to the small graveyard in back. He's sitting in the snow, leaning against a leafless tree, his legs stretched out in front of him. He's facing Father McMahon's headstone, the old schoolbag serving as an armrest. He looks up and musters a smile and a small wave as I approach.

"How long have you been sitting here?" I ask.

He checks his watch. "Sixty seconds or so."

I laugh. "You're in a time warp, Harry. I just left your apartment. I'd have seen you if you were only a minute ahead of me."

"I haven't been to my apartment yet," he says.

Harry spent last evening at the cottage with me. He opened a bottle of wine and boiled a couple of lobsters while I made a salad and sliced a loaf of sourdough. We ate a late dinner in the living room, close to the woodstove, and then decorated a Charlie Brown tree, one Harry had cut down in the woods behind the office. Luke got home at midnight and regaled us with tales of the fabulous young woman he'd just met—we have an endless supply in this town, it seems—before laughing out loud at our yuletide efforts. Harry left about an hour later and I assumed he was going home to bed, as any normal person would. I should know better by now.

I squat beside him, look closer at his face. He has the beginnings of a mustache and beard. His normally ruddy complexion is pale. And his eyes are bloodshot. "You haven't slept," I venture.

"Not yet," he says.

"Not yet? It's seven-thirty in the morning. What are you waiting for?"

"I've been busy."

"Doing what?"

He thinks about it for a few seconds. "Breaking and entering. In the night."

I stare at him.

"In a private dwelling," he adds.

"What the hell are you talking about, Harry?"

"I paid a little visit to Derrick Holliston's bachelor pad."

He can't be serious. "Holliston's been in the county jail for a year. Hasn't someone else rented that place by now?"

Harry shakes his head. "I worried about that too. I thought I'd have to knock on the door and introduce myself to the new tenant."

"What? You were planning to knock on a stranger's door in the wee hours of Christmas morning and ask if you could take a look around?"

He shrugs. "Turns out it wasn't necessary. A slightly overserved neighbor of his was just stumbling home when I got there. He said that unit's been vacant since the cops carted Holliston out of it. And once I got inside, I knew why. It's a dump."

"How'd you get in?"

He takes his left hand from his coat pocket; it's bandaged. "Broke a window in the kitchen door," he says. "It was pretty easy."

"What possessed you to use your hand?"

"I didn't," he says. "I used a brick. I cut the hand when I reached in to flip the deadlock."

"Cat Burglar of the Year?"

"It was dark," he says. "Could've happened to the best in the business."

I can't squat any longer—my middle-aged hips are complaining—so I kneel on the snow beside him. I'll have to put up with wet leggings for a while. "Help me out here, Harry. Why in God's name did you break into Holliston's old apartment?"

He reaches into his schoolbag and pulls out a sack—a faded blue pillowcase. "Go ahead," he says, "have a gander."

Cash. The bottom third of the pillowcase is filled with cold, hard cash—bills of almost all denominations. More ones than fifties, but plenty of everything in between too.

"The coins are on the bottom," Harry says, "mostly quarters. A year's worth of trips to the Laundromat."

"Let me guess." I tear my eyes from the mound of money and look back at him. "You're thinking this is last year's Christmas Eve collection."

"I'm not *thinking* anything," he says. "I know it is."

"You think it is, Harry, but you don't know it. You *can't* know it."

We seem to say that to each other a lot lately.

"Oh, yes, I can." He reaches into his schoolbag again, pulls out a second pillowcase—a mate of the first—and hands it over.

I know without looking, but I peer inside anyway, to make sure. And there it is: the monstrance. Tommy Fitzpatrick described it to a tee. A solid-gold stand, about a foot tall, its gleaming surface intricately carved. And the small, off-white wafer—the host—is still inside the monstrance's circular window. I look up at Harry and then back to the pillowcase. I'm numb, and it's not because of my wet knees. "The cops would've turned Holliston's apartment inside out looking for this evidence," I tell him. "Geraldine would have seen to that. How did you find it?"

He taps his temple. "Kidneys," he says. "Holliston told us he was an electrician in a prior life, remember?"

I'm blank for a few seconds, but then I do. Even so, I shake my head at Harry. "If Holliston's apartment has a suspended ceiling, you wouldn't be the only one to notice. The cops would have dismantled it first thing. That's Evidence Collection 101."

"It doesn't," he says. "The ceiling's plastered. And it's intact. Or it was, anyhow, until I got there."

It occurs to me that Harry probably needs a good lawyer. Maybe Bert Saunders is available. "What did you do to the ceiling?" I ask. I'm not sure I want to know, though.

"Took it down," he says.

"Took it *down*?"

"Not all of it."

Oddly enough, this doesn't make me feel much better.

"Just one corner," he adds. "The only spot that had been hollowed out."

I stare at him. Again.

"Holliston did a good job," he says. "I'll say that much for him. Maybe he was a plasterer in a prior life too."

I look down at the monstrance but don't say another word. I can't. The implications of this discovery are just beginning to hit me. I have to remind myself to breathe.

Approaching footsteps break the silence, the steady crunch of boots on snow. It's Monsignor Davis. He's in formal robes—it's Christmas, after all—but they're mostly hidden by a heavy gray coat. And his purple beanie has been replaced—or perhaps covered—by a warm woolen hat. "You're getting to be regulars around here," he says, smiling at us through the snowflakes.

"It's a temporary obsession," Harry tells him. "Don't go signing us up for catechism class."

The Monsignor laughs. "Don't worry," he says, "you'd scare the children."

"Now you've hurt my feelings." Harry wags a finger at the Monsignor as we both stand. "Not very Christian of you."

Monsignor Davis laughs again, shaking his head. "Paying a visit to Father McMahon?" he asks us.

Harry nods. "And to you, too, whether you like it or not." He holds out a pillowcase, the one full of money. "Here," he says, "this is yours. And I hope you'll believe me when I tell you I didn't have it until a couple of hours ago."

The Monsignor looks into the sack, then at me, then at Harry. "Glory be to God," he whispers. "What *is* this?"

Neither of us answers. We wait.

It takes about thirty seconds, but then his expression changes, the explanation dawning on him. "But there's no way to know," he says. "Is there?"

I hold out the second pillowcase and Monsignor Davis drops the bag of money on the snow. He looks inside the second sack, then at us, then back inside. He takes hold of the ornate gold stand and drops the empty pillowcase on top of the cash. His eyes are damp when he looks up. "Glory be to God," he whispers again.

We stand in silence for a few minutes, the Monsignor's eyes glued to the monstrance, the snow collecting on our hats and coats. "Justice," he says at last. "Another bit of justice for Father McMahon."

That's not true, of course. In the end, Derrick John Holliston is the only one who even came close to finding justice. He got exactly what the Constitution promises: he was judged by a jury of his peers, peers he pretty much hand-selected. Judge Gould sentenced him to twelve-to-fifteen on the voluntary manslaughter conviction. If he keeps his nose clean—and Holliston seems able to do that when he's on the inside—he'll be out in a decade. Francis Patrick McMahon didn't fare nearly as well.

"I'm sorry," Harry says, resting his bandaged hand on the Monsignor's shoulder, "about everything."

Monsignor Davis takes in the bandage, then looks closely at Harry's face. "Why don't you come to Mass?" he says. "Both of you. The eight o'clock starts in just a few minutes. Share your burdens with the good Lord."

Harry holds up both hands, palms out, to stop him. "I'm sorry, Your Emerald," he says, "but it's been sort of a rough morning. Could we not do the God thing right now?"

The Monsignor's laugh is hearty. He shakes Harry's hand, then mine. "All right," he says, "we'll do the God thing later."

Harry starts to protest, but the Monsignor cuts him off. "Whether you like it or not," he adds. He retrieves both pillow-cases and heads for the church's back door, the sack of money at his side, the monstrance pressed to his chest—no, to his heart.

"Hey, Padre," Harry calls after him.

Monsignor Davis stops on the bottom step and turns.

"Merry Christmas," Harry says.

The Monsignor nods, then smiles and disappears inside.

Harry retrieves his considerably lightened schoolbag and drapes his arm around my shoulders as we head for the cars. "Come back to Windmill Lane," I tell him. "Luke probably isn't up yet, but I've got eggs and bacon. He'll follow his nose downstairs as soon as we start cooking. After we eat, we can open presents."

Harry's expression brightens at once, and the change has nothing to do with gifts. Not the wrapped kind, anyway. "Eggs and bacon?" he says as he climbs into his Jeep. "It really *is* Christmas."

Luke's already up, as it turns out. I can tell by the thickness of the white smoke billowing from our brick chimney when I pull into the driveway. The woodstove was on a slow simmer when I left the cottage. It's cranking now.

His truck is parked next to my spot, buried under a foot of snow and blocked in by a silver Miata, its black retractable roof barely wet beneath a thin layer of the white stuff. It's a car that's normally garaged, apparently, and not one I recognize. Harry parks his Jeep behind my T-bird and eyes the Miata as he emerges. "Your son has a caller," he says as we head for the house, "and I'll bet the farm she's of the female persuasion."

He's right, of course. "Mom, Harry," Luke says when we come into the living room, "this is Chloe."

Chloe is the sweet young thing we heard about last night and she appears to be on her way out. They're both on their feet and she's zipping up her jacket. Luke didn't overstate his case; she's a knockout. Danny Boy is seated at her feet, panting up at her.

"Chloe," I say, "we're just about to make breakfast. Will you join us?"

Luke looks happy; I didn't say anything embarrassing, I guess.

"I would," she says, "but I promised my mom I'd be back to help with breakfast at home. We have a houseful. Thanks, though. I just came by to drop off a little present."

"Look," Luke says. "Chloe brought me this."

He holds up a pink box adorned with a brown ribbon, a combination near and dear to Chatham's locals and visitors alike. It's from the Candy Mansion, Chatham's source of all things sweet.

"Truffles," Luke says, and my mouth waters. The Candy Mansion's truffles are legendary. No doubt more than a few will disappear before we crack the first egg.

Luke and Danny Boy walk Chloe to the kitchen door. Luke's in sweats and socks, and Danny Boy has turned into a steadfast homebody in his old age, so neither of them is going any farther than that.

Harry manages to contain himself until the door slams shut, but then he lets out a loud whistle. He punches Luke on the arm—hard—when he rejoins us in the living room. "Nice work," Harry says. "And truffles to boot."

Luke shrugs and laughs, then looks down at his socks. He thinks he does nice work too, it seems.

Danny Boy barks, just once, and lifts his front paw to Harry's shin.

"Okay," Harry says, shaking the outstretched paw, "you do nice work too."

Danny Boy barks again, a happy one, and we all laugh. My son. And Danny Boy. The chick magnets.

Luke walks to the front window, pushes the lace curtain aside, and stares out into the driveway until we hear an ignition turn over. "Is she great," he says, turning back to face Harry and me, "or what?"

ABOUT THE AUTHOR

Rose Connors, whose debut novel, *Absolute Certainty,* won the Mary Higgins Clark Award, grew up in Philadelphia and received her law degree from Duke in 1984. A trial attorney for more than two decades, she is admitted to practice in both Washington State and Massachusetts. She lives on Cape Cod, where she spends summers commercial shell-fishing with her two teenage sons.